BEN BRIDGES

FLAME AND THUNDER

Complete and Unabridged

LINFORD
Leicester

First published in Great Britain in 2016

First Linford Edition
published 2018

A catalogue record for this book is available
from the British Library.

ISBN 978–1–4448–3757–5

Published by
F. A. Thorpe (Publishing)
Anstey, Leicestershire

Set by Words & Graphics Ltd.
Anstey, Leicestershire
Printed and bound in Great Britain by
T. J. International Ltd., Padstow, Cornwall

This book is printed on acid-free paper

1 899091 21

OCT

SPECIAL MESSAGE TO READERS

THE ULVERSCROFT FOUNDATION
(registered UK charity number 264873)

was established in 1972 to provide funds for research, diagnosis and treatment of eye diseases. Examples of major projects funded by the Ulverscroft Foundation are:-

- The Children's Eye Unit at Moorfields Eye Hospital, London
- The Ulverscroft Children's Eye Unit at Great Ormond Street Hospital for Sick Children
- Funding research into eye diseases and treatment at the Department of Ophthalmology, University of Leicester
- The Ulverscroft Vision Research Group, Institute of Child Health
- Twin operating theatres at the Western Ophthalmic Hospital, London
- The Chair of Ophthalmology at the Royal Australian College of Ophthalmologists

You can help further the work of the Foundation by making a donation or leaving a legacy. Every contribution is gratefully received. If you would like to help support the Foundation or require further information, please contact:

THE ULVERSCROFT FOUNDATION
The Green, Bradgate Road, Anstey
Leicester LE7 7FU, England
Tel: (0116) 236 4325

website: www.foundation.ulverscroft.com

FLAME AND THUNDER

It stands to be the biggest oil well in the territory, providing wildcatter Bud Bishop can bring it in before his lease runs out. However, Hugh Quillan wants to move in and keep the spoils for himself. So Bishop's backers hire freelance fighting man Carter O'Brien to keep Quillan's bullyboys in check. But the closer it comes to the deadline, the harder Quillan starts to play. With the threat of a full-scale war looming, O'Brien does the only thing he can — he makes sure his guns are loaded . . .

*For so many reasons,
this is for Janet*

1

When the body twitched a little, O'Brien realized it was still alive.

Seeing that, he heeled his horse back to speed, a solitary rider all but lost in the vast emptiness of the Kansas-Oklahoma border country until, at length, his shadow fell across the dying calf. The creature lay sprawled on its side in the middle of the plain, barely conscious and completely unaware of its surroundings. The most it could manage, as he swung down to inspect it, was a shallow, wheezing cough. There were no discernible wounds that he could see, only a brand that resembled an overturned shot glass containing the letter *M*.

A lean man of above average height, with rugged but not unpleasant features, O'Brien searched his surroundings through eyes the color of robins' eggs. He saw that the calf had come out of the low hills to the south, leaving a meandering set of tracks in its wake until it could walk no more.

Then the critter coughed again, and he realized that it had regained a hazy kind of focus, and was looking up at him with an expression that mixed confusion with hurt.

He'd just come from the White River country, where not so long before, the cattle industry had been decimated by an outbreak of hoof and mouth. Damned if he'd let the calf suffer any more than it had to, he tightened his grip on his horse's split reins and slid his Colt Lightning from the holster at his right hip.

Aiming at a spot between the creature's eyes, he pulled the trigger.

The echo of the shot rolled across the immensity of scrubby wheat-colored grass; and his horse, startled by the sound, jerked at the reins. Yanked sideways, O'Brien almost yelped, for he still hadn't finished healing from the beating he'd taken during the White

River business, a merciless rib-breaker that had come close to finishing him for good and all.

Head bent, senses swimming, he waited for the pain to subside.

Once it had, he slipped the gun away and checked his surroundings again, this time to see if the shot brought anyone running.

It didn't.

Gathering rein, he carefully remounted and rode on.

Not for the first time, he told himself that no sane man would have interrupted his convalescence to make a near-as-dammit six-hundred-mile trek to this desolate wilderness without good reason. But since the request to do so had come from a man he knew and respected, it had been hard to refuse. Besides, O'Brien was an adventurer by trade: taking it easy for any length of time didn't sit well with him and never had, no matter how attractive the woman who had taken it upon herself to nurse him back to health.

So when the telegram had caught up with him at Jane Farrow's ranch, O'Brien hadn't even needed to think about it. Within hours he'd said his goodbyes to the friends he'd made there and was on his way to the Kansas border country.

Although a spider's web of railroad spurs and feeders had taken much of the strain out of the journey, it had soon become evident that he was still nowhere near as spry as a professional fighting man ought to be. Reluctant though he was to admit it, it was taking ever longer to heal now that he was well into his forties. But there could be no turning back now: turning back didn't sit well with him, either.

Besides, he was curious. He'd neither seen nor heard from Aaron Norris in years, and wondered why the congressman had need of him now.

The telegram itself had only given him the basics. NEED YOUR HELP SOONEST STOP MEET TEMPLE SUNFLOWER HOTEL SUNRISE

KANS STOP NORRIS. Perhaps deliberately, there'd been no indication as to what he might be getting into.

He was still pondering that when, twenty minutes later, a poor excuse for a trail led him to a thin stream shaded by Shumard oak and redbud. Here, his aching bones finally convinced him to rest up a while.

Dismounting, he loosened the cinches on his old Texas double-rig, then unbit the horse so that it could graze. With the horse tended to, he dug a shallow pit on the bank of the creek, threw in some dry grass and freshly sliced bark for kindling, and lit a small fire. While that took hold, he went to fill his coffee-pot.

One look at the stream, however, made him think again. The water had a greasy, unappetizing appearance to it. And when he studied his surroundings more closely, he saw that the arrowhead and cattails, duckweed and water primroses that lined both banks were either dead or dying.

Thumbing his Stetson back off his cropped salt-and-pepper hair, he wondered if the calf had drunk here; if this water had somehow caused its —

That was when he caught the sound of hooves coming fast from the north, and turned as a rider galloped into sight through the trees.

Seeing the campsite ahead of him, the newcomer brought his strawberry roan to a rump-sliding halt, leapt from his saddle while the animal was still in motion, and with work spurs jingling, hurriedly began to stamp O'Brien's fire out before it could take hold.

Puzzled — and that was putting it mildly — O'Brien came back from the creek, instinctively transferring the coffeepot from his right hand to his left.

The shorter, stockier man was too busy killing the fire to notice the cautionary movement. Only when he was satisfied that the fire was out did he look up, the broad shoulders beneath his buttoned box jacket rising and falling with the effort he'd just put into the task.

'Damn you!' he snapped, his square jaw stiff with anger. 'Ain't you got the sense you was born with?'

Temper boiling over, he launched himself at O'Brien with a wide-looping roundhouse right.

Instinctively O'Brien brought the coffeepot up, and there came a heavy clang of sound as the newcomer's knuckles met its hard granite surface. The man flinched as pain shot up his arm, and before he could recover, O'Brien jabbed him in the face with his bunched right.

The man spilled over, squirmed in the grass.

'Sonofabitch!' he managed at last, and as he said it, his hand, with its rapidly swelling knuckles, slid toward the looped-down Peacemaker sitting high on his waist.

O'Brien's own .38 was cocked almost faster than thought. 'Don't,' he advised.

Awed by the speed of the draw, the other man didn't. He slowly, cautiously brought his hand away from the gun.

7

'Sonofabitch!' he said again. But after that, the anger leeched from his acorn-brown eyes, and he looked madder at himself than at the man who'd just decked him.

O'Brien figured he was about fifty or so, clean-shaven and with moderately handsome still-boyish features. He wore bull-hide chaps over black canvas work pants, and his short hair, now that his sweat-darkened Stetson had tumbled away, showed dusty blond. Shaking his injured fist to get some feeling back into it, he muttered a heartfelt, 'Damn.'

'You'll live,' O'Brien decided.

'Yeah,' the man agreed sourly. 'But if I hadn't come along when I did, *you* might not've.'

Seeing O'Brien freeze in the act of returning his Colt to leather, he went on irritably, 'Ah, it wasn't meant as a threat, so don't take it as such.' And without warning he added, 'Was it you killed my calf back a ways?'

'Is that what this is all about?'

'*Was* it you?' the man prodded.

'If your brand's Rolling M, then yeah — it was me.'

He braced himself for the other's reaction. But when it came, it wasn't what he'd been expecting.

'Thanks,' the man said quietly.

As satisfied as he could be that the newcomer no longer posed a threat, O'Brien returned to his horse, shoved the coffee-pot into one saddlebag and took out a half-empty bottle of Forty Rod. 'Here,' he said, offering it by the neck.

Surprised by the offer, the man sat up a little straighter, deliberately keeping his movements slow and easy as he took the bottle. Following an experimental sniff at the strong whiskey, he took a pull, grimaced and then took one more.

'I guess I owe you an apology,' he muttered at last.

'I guess you do.'

'Well, I was at fault, an' I'm man enough admit it. I don't usually ruffle so easy, but — let's just say it's been a tough few months.' He wiped a hand across his mouth, wincing a little because his bottom lip had swollen as well. 'I heard the shot, found the calf, figured I'd catch up and thank you for what you did — puttin' it out of its misery, I mean. 'Course, when I saw the fire . . . '

'So let's start over,' said O'Brien.

The other man nodded. He offered his hand and introduced himself as Lon McPhail. O'Brien took the hand, they shook, and while O'Brien still had a grip on him he pulled McPhail back to his feet before giving his own name. 'What happened to your calf, anyway?' he asked.

'That I can't say for sure,' replied McPhail, scooping up his hat, punching it back into shape and setting it back on his head, 'but I can guess well enough.' Meaningfully, he cut his gaze toward the creek.

'The water?'

'What's *in* the water,' said McPhail, and making it sound like a cuss-word he added: '*Oil*.'

'There's no wildcatting in these parts, is there?'

'In these parts there doesn't have to be,' McPhail grumbled. 'But they're drillin', all right. 'Bout fifteen miles south.'

Now it was O'Brien's turn to show surprise. 'And what happens fifteen miles south affects you here?'

'Way I understand it,' explained the rancher, 'a man can drill for oil just about anyplace he likes, but if he goes too deep an' cracks the caprock, there can be hell to pay for miles around.'

'I still don't get it.'

McPhail thought a moment. 'Say a man drillin' for oil opens up a pocket of gas instead,' he replied. 'He does that, the gas can rise up through the ground, an' sometimes find its way into the water, like it's done in this creek here. The cows drink the water 'cause they don't know any different, an' then they take sick an' die.'

Grasping that, O'Brien made a further, chilling connection. 'So if I'd let my fire take hold just now . . . '

McPhail nodded. 'Slightest spark could've ignited the gas an' oil in the water,' he confirmed. 'It's happened before — I've seen it. Never seen fire like it, either, the way it burns so fierce. That's why I guess I got so nettled.'

'Then it's *me* who's obliged to *you*,' O'Brien said, meaning it.

McPhail figured that gave him the right to indicate O'Brien's tied-down holster. 'You're mighty slick with that smoke-wheel,' he remarked, his tone elaborately casual. 'Passin' through, are you?'

'Headed for a town called Sunrise.'.

'Is that what they're callin' it these days?' asked McPhail, and he made a disparaging *pshaw* sound. 'Well, if that's the case, I can tell you right now it's the sorriest excuse for a town that ever bore the name. Not much more'n a collection of tents and shanties; here today, gone tomorrow — gone tomorrow if we're lucky.'

'What's wrong with it?'

McPhail considered a reply, then shook his head. 'Ah, pay me no mind. Just the whiskey talkin', is all.' But a new thought had just occurred to him. 'What takes you to Sunrise Ranch, anyway?'

'A job.'

'Workin' for Graves?'

'Who's Graves?'

'You've never heard of Elijah Graves?'

'Nope.'

'Quillan, then?'

'Never heard of him, either,' said O'Brien. 'Tell you the truth, McPhail, I don't even know what the job is yet, much less whether or not I'll take it.'

'Then maybe I can offer you somethin' better,' the rancher said impulsively.

'Oh?'

'I'll lay it out straight as I can,' McPhail continued, his manner wholly grim now. 'I been lookin' to hire a man who's good with a gun. No offense, but you got the look of such a man. Am I right?'

Wondering if McPhail's proposal

13

might have anything to do with his own business out here, O'Brien said carefully, 'Maybe.'

'You interested?'

'I'll hear you out, sure. But no promises.'

'Fair enough,' said McPhail. 'Here's the short of it. The town you call Sunrise used to be the Sunrise Ranch, till Elijah Graves quit the ranchin' business an' opened up his land to oil speculators.'

'What made him think he had oil?'

'Hell, man, where we stand right now, we're barely a hoot an' a holler from the border with Indian Territory! They been usin' oil over there for more'n twenty years.'

O'Brien knew that: knew also that when first discovered, no one had really known what to do with the stuff, which had been known as 'rock oil' back then. Eventually the Indians had started using it as cheap illuminating fuel, and after a time began selling it to the whites for much the same purpose.

Pretty soon thereafter, the distillated by-product, kerosene, had replaced whale oil in lanterns right across the country.

'Now,' McPhail went on, 'they say oil's the comin' thing — an' it's hard to argue when you see what's already happened in places like Nacogdoches, an' the San Joaquin Valley, in California. The demand's growing because they say it can be used to run machinery an' such — an' I guess Graves figured that the man who gets in early enough stands to make the most money from the demand for it. So he hired a bunch of . . . geologicalists, I think they was called . . . to come take a look around Sunrise, an' they reckoned the land showed promise.'

'But rather than drill for it himself . . . ?'

'Graves wanted a sure-fire thing, not a gamble. So he sold leases on the land. No matter what happens now, he's richer'n a fat chef's fruitcake. Trouble is, the promise of oil — just the promise of it, mind, no guarantees of actually strikin' it — was enough to draw every two-legged vulture for miles around.'

'And they're giving you trouble, these vultures?' prodded O'Brien. 'Aside from poisoning your water, I mean?'

McPhail looked like he wanted to chew nails and spit rust. 'Since Sunrise started callin' itself a town, we've had a rustlin' problem that jus' won't go away,' he said. 'A big one, that's like to put us smaller ranchers out of business for good if it carries on. You ask me, someone in that hell-hole's responsible for it, an' someone else must be turnin' a blind eye to let 'em get away with it.'

'Have you told Graves?'

'That was the first thing all us ranchers did. But Graves won't do anythin' that might stop the money rollin' in.'

'That's rough.'

'You're damn right it is. Graves always was the lead steer in these parts, but there was never any meanness in him. If we ever needed extra grass or water, he was always the first to give it. But not anymore, not since he hired Quillan. No friends in the oil business, I guess.'

'So you're looking to hire someone to solve your rustling problem.'

'That's it. Someone who can look after himself, use a gun, like I say, an' play rough when he needs to.' He waited for that to sink in, then said, 'Pay you well for your time, too, O'Brien. None of us alone could afford it, but if we all chip in . . . '

'You'd do better to hire a range detective,' O'Brien told him.

'Daresay. But that takes time. An' you're already here.'

O'Brien reflected on what he'd heard. There was trouble in these parts, then, and the dealing with and settling of trouble was his business. But rustling . . . was that was why Aaron Norris had asked him to come out to Sunrise? Knowing Norris, he felt sure it must be something more than that.

McPhail, meanwhile, was waiting to

hear his decision. He said, 'Tell you what I'll do, McPhail. I'll hear the other feller out, and if I don't care much for the sound of his job, I might just come back and take you up on yours.'

It wasn't the answer the rancher wanted, but he put a brave face on it. 'Good enough,' he said. 'But I'll tell you now, O'Brien, we're the better bet. When they drill for oil, they kill the land. The grass withers, the water spoils, the cattle die. But oil'll come an' go. There'll always be a need for beef — and men to stop it being stolen.'

'I believe you.'

McPhail offered his hand again. 'If you got any sense,' he said, 'you'll avoid Sunrise altogether, an' come look me up at the Rollin' M. I got me a bad feelin' about that 'town' of yours. They's trouble brewin' there, O'Brien — bad trouble. An' sooner or later folks're gonna start turnin' up dead, just to prove it.'

2

He *felt* the town before he saw it.

He felt it in the steady, remorseless pounding of more heavy iron bits than he could possibly estimate, and knew that somewhere up ahead each pile-driver blow was hammering a questing drill that little bit deeper into rock or through soil, and sending out waves of sound to make the ground vibrate beneath him.

It was the very heartbeat of Sunrise he was feeling — the seemingly endless boring of well holes that might at any moment spell success for their operators . . . or complete failure.

A half-mile on he *heard* the town, as well.

It buzzed with the constant growl and splutter of donkey engines and the eternal nauseating *thump . . . thump . . . thump* that now accompanied every shiver in the ground.

A few moments later he topped a long hogback ridge and drew rein, for neither feeling nor sound could have prepared him for what lay ahead — a veritable forest of derricks spread across an area miles wide, each one spearing seventy to a hundred feet toward the overcast sky.

Each structure was a bewildering four-sided network of sturdy wooden beams and rope, leather, canvas and iron, each cable-festooned face tapering gradually toward the pinnacle, every one marking the spot where Elijah Graves had sold a lease for God alone knew how much.

By O'Brien's estimate there were at least eighty of them, some set apart from the rest, others standing almost shoulder to shoulder across the once-pristine plain. They were nearly all built to the same pattern: most had one platform about midway to the top, and another — more of a crow's nest, really — just shy of the summit. And at the base of each there stood a chaotic jumble of rough-cut lumber and resin pipes, folded tarpaulins, spare or broken iron bits and wagons parked next to open-sided engine houses or storage sheds. Steam-driven walking beams, situated at the foot and to one side of every derrick, seesawed back and forth, back and forth, hammering continuously at temper screws, the screws in turn beating jars, augur stems and finally the center-bits themselves into the ground.

It looked like something straight out of hell.

A breeze blew up then, and at last O'Brien got his first *smell* of Sunrise. It was a sickening blend of sap and garbage, of man-sweat, poor sanitation and, curiously, a stench not unlike burnt guttapercha. Sunrise smelled of fires old and not so old, of grease and natural gas, sulfur and gypsum. And overlaying it all was the sickly sweet stink of raw — what some men called crude — oil that had already been coaxed to the surface.

He gave the blood-bay his heels and the horse descended the facing slope and then, at his bidding, swung a wide loop toward the town itself, which lay mercifully upwind of the massive oil field. But as he skirted the eastern fringe of the field he noticed that one of the derricks had partially collapsed, and was now little more than a pile of fire-blackened beams that still smoldered, popped and glowed orange every time the wind hit them just right.

He slowed his pace. A crowd of men in stained coveralls had gathered around the wreckage, some trying to salvage what they could, others holding their hats in hand and muttering darkly among themselves. Beyond them, just to one side of the charred, now-roofless storage shed, he saw a body beneath a canvas sheet, a red stain covering most of the off-white material where the chest would be.

A big, towheaded man in his late forties, dressed in oil-stained blue coveralls, was standing beside the corpse. A smaller, older man in a creased gray suit with a silver badge pinned to his lapel was addressing him earnestly, but the towhead, ashen-faced and glassy-eyed, was hardly even aware of him. A glossy black water spaniel, sitting beside the lawman, occasionally glanced up at him sadly.

O'Brien wondered what had happened to destroy the derrick. Accidents were hardly uncommon in places like this, of course. They went with the territory. But the corpse under the blanket, leaking blood from some kind of chest wound, made him wonder if there was more to this particular 'accident' than met the eye.

I got me a bad feelin' about that 'town' of yours, McPhail had told him. They's trouble brewin' there, O'Brien — bad trouble. An' sooner or later folks're gonna start turnin' up dead, just to prove it.

O'Brien wondered if just maybe they already were.

$\star$ $\star$ $\star$

He soon realized that McPhail had been right about something else, too — Sunrise really *was* the sorriest excuse for a town he'd ever seen.

Flanking both sides of a central, wheel-rutted main street, it was a muddle of hastily erected board buildings and wall tents, a few corrugated iron shanties — mostly temporary saloons or eateries — and even some prefabricated buildings that must have been shipped in from the east and erected on site in a day or less. Parked wagons of varying makes occupied all remaining space, many flying the Stars and Stripes, or wind-ruffled banners proclaiming the likes of Steve's Cream Soda, General Merchandise, Ice-Cold Beer or Real New York Victuals.

Here a sign maker worked hard with brush and paint to keep up with demand, there a short, portly man in a dusty pulpit gown tried to encourage passers-by into his open-air Presbyterian church.

Next door, a one-sheet newspaper called the *Sunrise Journal* operated from the back of an old Rocker ambulance. And between all these disparate establishments lay a network of puddle-filled side streets, most overlaid with planks at corners and junctions to make rough-and-ready crossing points.

The street itself was jammed with wagons, riders and pedestrians, all of which slowed his progress to a crawl.

'You lookin' for a deal on some land, mister? Here, step down a while and I'll tell you all you need to know!'

'You, sir! Did you know that drinking leads to neglect of duty, moral degradation and crime? Please, come and sign the pledge of the Women's Christian Temperance Union!'

O'Brien bypassed them all.

Most of the pedestrians were tough-looking men in coveralls, but there was also a scattering of businessmen, some dandily-dressed gamblers, heavy-set freighters, a few cowboys hazing cows stamped with clumsily blotted brands to one eatery or another, and even the odd pigtailed Celestial, picking his way nimbly through the crowds. There were women, too, O'Brien saw, though not the prim and proper ladies of the WCTU. These were the kind that always found a living in mining towns and oil-camps like this one, and they looked as rough and tough as the wildcatters themselves.

He continued to walk his mount along the main thoroughfare, his eyes moving from left to right and back again as he sought his destination. He saw dry goods stores and barbershops, blacksmiths, drug stores and meat markets, but overwhelmingly he saw saloons and so-called 'oilfield harems', and even at this time of day they were all doing good business.

The most impressive saloon was a place called The Christmas Tree, a prefabricated structure two stories high, which boasted its own shaded porch at the front, and dusty, real glass windows flanking an ornately carved set of batwing doors.

O'Brien's destination, the Sunflower Hotel, stood directly opposite, and after The Christmas Tree was probably the most impressive structure Sunrise had to offer. Like The Christmas Tree, it was also a two-story board-and-batten structure, but this one had small, smeared windows and a sheet metal roof, which likely turned the rooms into ovens on hot days.

Dismounting gratefully out front, he eased the knots from his spine, tied up at the hitch rack and headed for the open doorway.

The reception area beyond was no more than a ring-marked desk and a chair set to one side of what looked to be a very rickety staircase. A thin, long-necked man in shirtsleeves was sitting at the desk, idly watching the comings and goings of the people on the street. The moment O'Brien came inside he called, 'We're full.'

'I'm not looking for a room,' O'Brien replied without breaking stride. 'Just a man.'

'Oh?'

'Name of Temple.'

The clerk nodded. 'The lawyer.'

'If you say so. Is he here?'

'I'm here,' called a voice from the top of the stairs.

Stepping back a pace, O'Brien looked up to see a pale, studious man around thirty or so, dressed in well-tailored gray suit pants and a boiled white shirt beneath a matching two-pocket vest.

'And you are . . . ?' the man asked expectantly.

'O'Brien.'

Showing relief, the man hurried downstairs, each tread creaking beneath him even though he was below average height and hardly overweight. He had a serious oval-shaped face with perceptive gray eyes, and his trimmed chevron mustache was, like his short neatly barbered hair, as black as licorice.

'I'm Jim Temple,' he said as he reached the foot of the staircase and offered his right hand. 'Thank you for — '

He bit off then, as he got a better look at O'Brien and saw the true extent of his still-battered appearance.

'I, ah . . . think there . . . might have been some mistake,' he said uncomfortably, withdrawing his hand.

A smile showed sparingly at O'Brien's mouth. 'Do tell.'

Temple glanced at the desk clerk, then lowered his voice. 'We sent for a fighting man,' he said. 'If you'll forgive me for saying so, Mr. O'Brien, you look more like a man who's just been in a fight.'

Although O'Brien was too old a hand to take it personally, his eyes hardened a little when he said, softly, 'Seems to me you're judging the book by its cover, Mr. Temple.'

'I'm — '

'Quillan!'

The name, yelled by someone out on the street, stopped Temple in his tracks. He brushed past O'Brien and went to the door just in time to see the crowds outside parting hurriedly for the big towheaded man in blue coveralls O'Brien had seen out at the burned derrick. Temple muttered something under his breath, then said urgently, 'Come here, Mr. O'Brien! I think you should see this.'

O'Brien joined him. As he did so, a big black man in the crowd tried to grab the towhead's shirtsleeve and hold him back, but the towhead was having none of it. Angrily he shrugged out of the other man's grip and kept going, everything about him speaking of anger and determination as he hauled up in front of The Christmas Tree.

'Who is that feller?' asked O'Brien.

'That's Jeff Jenner. His lease got firebombed last night.'

O'Brien nodded. 'I passed it on the way in. And Quillan?'

'Quillan,' Temple said in an undertone, as the clerk came to join them in the doorway, 'is the reason we sent for you.'

Outside, Jenner again yelled, 'Quillan!'

A quiet had come over the street, and

though he knew it was only his imagination, O'Brien felt that even the persistent *thump . . . thump . . . thump . . .* of the derricks had suddenly diminished.

'Quillan!' yelled Jenner. 'Get out here! I got business with you!'

The spectators stood in silence, watching, waiting. Nothing happened immediately. Then, from inside the saloon, O'Brien heard the slow, steady sound of footsteps on sawdust-covered duckboards coming closer. Moments later, the batwings pushed open and a tall well-built man came outside.

'That's him,' whispered Temple. 'Hugh Quillan.'

Quillan was dressed in a fine black suit and a brocade vest, his ruddy face just a little too fleshy to be handsome, his curly brown hair well barbered, his lively green eyes filled with confidence. His jaw was strong and dimpled, and the promise of a smile played constantly at his mouth, showing him to be a man of easy humor who didn't let a whole lot trouble him. He was about forty, powerful with it, and still very much in shape.

A second man had followed Quillan outside, equally tall but much leaner. While Quillan stepped down into the street, however, the second man merely leaned his narrow shoulders against the wall to one side of the fancy batwings, a black-paper cigarette dangling from the corner of his mouth. He was dark and bristly, about the same age as Quillan, but with a thinner face, a longer nose and very dark, nervy eyes that constantly shuttled from Quillan to the towhead who'd challenged him. He wore a checked shirt tucked into pale yellow nankeen pants, the pants in turn tucked into well-worn stovepipe boots. A gun hung low at his left hip, a single-action Remington Army .45, and his palm constantly brushed against it.

Quillan, now in the center of the street, considered Jenner for a long moment. Since all eyes were on him, he clearly intended to put on a show. The near-silence stretched interminably, until at last Quillan, his Irish brogue as thick as a ten-dollar steak, said, 'Keep it down to a dull roar, if ye please, Jenner. Some of us here are trying to play cards.'

'Damn you and your cards!' snarled Jenner. 'You've overstepped the mark this time, damn you! You couldn't buy us out, you couldn't scare us out, and I'm damned if I'll let you burn us out!'

Quillan raised his eyebrows, overplaying his bafflement for the benefit of the onlookers. 'I don't know what you're talking about,' he said. His tone, however, said that he knew exactly what Jenner was talking about: that everyone knew what he was talking about; and that he, Quillan, didn't give a damn.

'Then you're a dirty, stinking liar!' called Jenner. 'Worse than that, you're a murderer!'

A gasp whispered through the crowd.

'Am I, now?' asked Quillan.

Jenner stabbed a finger back the way he'd come. 'My brother Billy died trying to fight that fire you started! 'Fore he could even get close to that blaze with the hose, someone shot him! Shot him from the shadows and killed him stone dead!'

In the distance, the derricks went on *thump . . . thump . . . thumping*.

'And you're saying that was me?' Quillan prompted.

'It was done on your say-so!' Jenner roared. 'And in my book that makes you responsible!'

Quillan shrugged. 'Well, you swear out a complaint against me and I'll answer it in a court o' law. But without evidence, you're wasting your time and mine.'

He started to turn away. For Jenner, already strung out tight, that was the last straw. He fumbled an old Webley Bull Dog revolver from the pocket of his coveralls.

'Don't you turn your back on me, you sonofabitch!'

Quillan faced him again. 'Don't be a damn fool,' he said, not in the least bit fazed by the small but deadly gun pointed at him. 'Swear out a complaint with Marshal Chamberlain, if ye have to. But ye aim a gun at me, ye'd best be prepared to use it.'

'Oh, I'll use it, all right,' said Jenner.

Quillan stared at him for a deathly silent moment. Then, almost to himself, he said, 'Aye. Just maybe ye will.'

And then, shockingly sudden, Quillan's own hands flipped back the folds of his frock coat, revealing a tooled black leather belt hung with two holsters, and then the hands were filled with guns — twin Cavalry Colts — and each one was spitting flame.

O'Brien had never seen a faster draw.

Hit twice, Jenner took a couple of ill-coordinated steps backward, his own gun unfired. Then he buckled and splashed heavily into the mud. Some-one in the crowd — it was the big black man again — yelled his name, but by then Jenner was beyond hearing. There was a single blotch of blood on the front of his coveralls, surprisingly small, and a second right between his shock-wide eyes. He lay with his arms stretched out to either side of him, staring blindly at the overcast sky.

The derricks went on *thump, thump, thumping* . . .

'You sonofabitch!' someone in the crowd yelled.

Sliding his Colts back into leather, Quillan looked around for the speaker. Unable to pinpoint him, he addressed the crowd in general. 'T'was a fair fight!' he called easily. 'Ye all saw that!'

An ominous murmur ran through some of the men toward the back of the gathering. They wanted to tell Quillan that it had been no such thing — that he was a man who made his living with his guns, while Jenner had been a wildcatter who'd only ever held a weapon by the barrel so he could use the butt for a hammer. But no one said anything.

'It was self-defense,' Quillan added.

Still no one spoke.

His white, even teeth flashed in a grin, and then he turned and started back toward the saloon. He got as far as the boardwalk and then the thin man with the very dark eyes plucked the black-paper cigarette from his mouth, leaned forward and said something through a haze of expelled smoke. Frowning, Quillan turned, sought out and found Temple, and when his green eyes moved to O'Brien they narrowed an infinitesimal fraction more.

He came back down into the street and crossed over to the hotel, striding chin-up and confident. Away to his left, a couple of wildcatters broke through the crowd, then set about dragging Jenner's body away. At the rack, O'Brien's horse sidestepped a little, unnerved by the shooting and the man who'd done it.

'Too bad ye had to see that, Temple,' Quillan called by way of greeting. 'I know ye've no stomach for that kinda thing.'

Temple made a meaningless gesture with one hand. 'I'll get over it,' he said in a choked tone. 'Which is more than I can say for that poor soul.'

'That 'pour soul', as ye call him, was

out to do me harm,' said Quillan reasonably. 'And ye know the way things are out here. Ye bite or ye get bit. And I'm not about to get bit — by anyone.' His eyes moved to O'Brien. 'Who's your friend here?'

'Just that,' said Temple. 'A friend.'

Quillan offered his name, but only so he could get O'Brien's in return. Meeting Quillan's gaze, O'Brien told him.

'Seems to me I've heard of you,' said Quillan, having given it a moment's thought. 'If you're the same O'Brien, that is. They say you're a gun-for-hire.'

'Is that what they say?'

'They say ye sell your gun when the job and the money are right. That what brings you to Sunrise, O'Brien? Work? I can always find a use for a good man, especially with such a fine Irish-soundin' name as your own.' He eyed O'Brien insolently, taking in the healing bruises, the swelling that still persisted along his brow, around his mouth. ''Course,' he added, 'ye look a little sorry for yerself right now.'

'I'm just here, visiting friends.'

'Like your man, Temple, here?'

'Yep. Just like Temple, here.'

'Anyone else?'

'Nobody you'd know.'

'Bishop?' asked Quillan.

'Don't know anyone by that name,' O'Brien answered honestly.

'Well, happen ye should run into him, be sure an' pass along my regards,' said Quillan.

'I'll do that,' said O'Brien. Gesturing to the men carrying Jenner away, he said, 'What was that all about?'

'You heard him. He said I burned down his rig.'

'*Did* you?'

A nerve above Quillan's right eye twitched. 'That's a hell of an unfriendly question to ask.'

'It's a hell of an unfriendly thing to do.'

'Well, I'll tell ye,' said Quillan, conversationally now. 'I get a problem with someone, I face 'em straight up. I don't do what Jenner accused me of doing.'

'I believe you, Quillan. But that's not

to say you don't order it done.'

Quillan's eyes went flat this time, and once again the lids came down a notch. 'You're tryin' awful hard to say somethin', I'm thinkin'.'

'Well, that weasel-faced *hombre* on the boardwalk yonder. That's Nate Newton, isn't it?'

'You know Nate?'

'No, but I know of him. And I know there's nothing he won't do for money.'

'Then maybe you ought to take that up with Nate.'

'Sure,' said O'Brien. 'Send him over. I'll ask him straight up.'

For a moment Quillan looked as if he might just do that. He was curious to see what would happen. But then he changed his mind. He knew Nate. He didn't know O'Brien. And that being the case, there was no forecasting the outcome. Instead he said, 'You're awful sure of yerself, O'Brien.'

'It's the only way to be,' O'Brien replied.

'Well, I'll be seein' ye around — that

is, if you're stayin' for any length of time.'

'You never know.'

Quillan smiled again, then turned and walked slowly back over to the saloon. Nate Newton stood beside the batwings, the cigarette dangling from the corner of his mouth again, his dark eyes shuttling from Quillan to O'Brien.

'You're right about Newton,' Temple said in an undertone. 'He's a dirty, rotten back-shooter. And when Quillan tells him what you called him, it's *your* back he'll be shooting at. That wasn't why we asked you here.'

O'Brien turned to him. 'Then why did you?'

Temple studied him a moment. 'Let's not waste each other's time, Mr. O'Brien. Now that I've seen you, I'm not sure you're really up to this job. We're in a rough situation here, and it's likely to get rougher before it's through. Now, you're obviously still nursing injuries from some previous escapade. That puts you at risk — and it puts us at risk, too, if we have to rely on you.'

'I can't fault your reasoning, Temple. I *am* stove up. But why don't you tell me what it is you need from me, and then let me be the judge of whether or not I can handle it?'

Temple drew air in through his nostrils. 'If it was up to me, I'd tell you to turn around, ride back where you came from and finish healing,' he replied. 'But . . . '

'But?'

'Congressman Norris speaks highly of you, so out of respect for him . . . ' He reached a decision, though he was clearly unhappy with it. 'All right,' he said with new purpose. 'I'll grant you that much. You've come a far piece, I imagine, but . . . are you up to a little more riding?'

'Sure.'

'Then let me grab my hat and jacket and rent a horse. I won't tell you what this is all about — I'll show you.'

3

'As I understand it,' Temple said as the town fell behind them, 'Congressman Norris got into some sort of scrape down in Mexico a few years ago, and you got him out of it.'

'Something like that,' O'Brien replied. His interest had been taken by a scattering of crude wooden crosses spread across some flat land a hundred yards or so behind the town — Sunrise's sadly overstocked cemetery.

'Client confidentiality, is that it?' prompted Temple, astride a placid sorrel he'd rented from a makeshift corral next door to the hotel.

O'Brien shrugged. 'If you mean it's nobody's business but the congressman's, you're right. Besides, there's not that much to tell.'

'That's not Aaron's opinion. Whatever it was that happened south of the border, he never forgot you.'

'Where are we headed, anyway?' O'Brien asked to change the subject.

'You'll see,' Temple replied, and was unable to resist adding, 'You're not the only one who can keep secrets around here, Mr. O'Brien.'

O'Brien had been expecting them to head back toward the forest of derricks he'd passed on the way in. Instead, Temple led them south, away from town and on across country that was mostly short-grass plains and scrub, separated by rolling hills, ridges and low mountains. Trees were relatively sparse here, but still O'Brien noted occasional stands of red cedar, piñon pine and ponderosa, and knew that this had once been good ranchland. Now, however, the grass had a brittle, sickly look to it, and the heavy clouds that always seemed to form over oilfields did little to make it look any healthier.

When at length they came to a ragged waterhole surrounded by rocks and overshadowed by a slope studded with black walnut, he saw the same greasy film overlaying the surface of the water, and began to get an idea of just how widespread the damage caused by drilling could be.

At the crest of the rise he found himself overlooking another vast tree-bordered meadow of washed-out grass . . . and a single derrick that stood *thump, thump, thumping* on the horizon.

Drawing rein, Temple said, 'Mr. O'Brien — say hello to Kathryn.'

'Kathryn?'

'Otherwise known as the Bishop well.'

O'Brien studied the place with hands crossed over his saddlehorn. There wasn't much to set it apart from any of the other wells he'd seen so far, except its out-of-the-way location. The lease was bordered by piles of cut lumber and resin pipes, a Conestoga wagon beside a crudely built corral in which a few horses rolled or wandered, and various stores or equipment stacked here and there beneath work-stained tarpaulins. The derrick at its center stood around a hundred feet tall, an intricate lacework of beams and bolts, at the foot of which stood a walking beam beside an engine house. A wall tent, its sides rolled up to give the interior an airing, showed where the hired men slept: O'Brien assumed that Bishop himself probably lived in the timber-fronted dugout carved into the shallow hill to the east.

'Come on,' said Temple. 'Let's go on down.'

A man halfway up the derrick saw them coming while they were still a ways out, and called down to a man in a derby hat, who was working the walking beam. Derby Hat didn't hear him at first. The constant pounding of the drill and the nearer flapping and snapping of cables drowned everything else out. Then, catching the second warning, he turned, snatched up a nearby carbine and hopped down off the platform to come out and intercept them. Three other men also stopped work and clustered in a group to watch what happened next.

When Derby Hat was no more than a dozen feet away, Temple drew rein and O'Brien followed suit. Recognizing the attorney, Derby Hat's grip on the carbine relaxed a touch, but his expression remained suspicious as he eyed O'Brien.

'Mr. Temple,' said the man, nodding.

'Bud,' replied Temple. 'I'd like you to meet Carter O'Brien. O'Brien's the man Congressman Norris sent for. O'Brien — Bud Bishop.'

Short and leather-skinned, Bud Bishop wore mud-stained canvas pants and a blue shirt that struggled to accommodate his generous belly. Atop his coarse, silver-streaked hair he wore his derby hat at an impudent jack-deuce angle. He was pushing sixty, O'Brien guessed, but he was still undeniably tough. The oft-broken nose that occupied the center of his flushed face looked more like a pitted strawberry, and it overhung a wide, intractable mouth. But there was humor in his dark eyes, which were all but lost in fans of wrinkles.

While they sized each other up, the man who'd raised the alarm in the first place came down off the rig with the ease of a monkey. As he hurried to join them, O'Brien was struck by just how much he resembled Bishop. His lean, muscular body had yet to run to fat, of course, and the lines of his face were somewhat softer, his skin less sun-worn, his brown eyes affable and not nearly so worldly. He was about half Bishop's age, a little taller, and his hair was a dustier, shorter blond.

'Mr. Temple,' he hailed, striding up.

'My son, Don,' introduced Bud. 'And that there,' he added, 'is Don's wife, Kath.'

O'Brien had seen the half-glazed dugout door open as they rode up. But the woman who now walked unhurriedly toward them was a revelation. The breeze plastered her cheap, flowery dress to the contours of a slender, long-legged body, and whispered through her long blond hair, which the sun had bleached to light ivory. Her heart-shaped face tapered to a strong, pointed jaw, and her blue eyes surveyed him from almond-shaped sockets. When she smiled at him, her full lips pulled back to show fine teeth with an appealing hint of overbite. She was, he thought, about twenty-five, twenty-six.

'This here's Mr. O'Brien,' said Don, sliding an arm around her waist and hugging her to him. 'The congressman's man.'

She was almost the same height as Don. 'Welcome,' she said, appraising him.

The introductions made, Bishop invited them down, and once they'd tied their horses to the top corral post, and the other men had been told to get back to work, they joined the Bishops in the dugout.

It was a small, shadowy oblong of a place with dirt walls and a dirt floor, the two sleeping areas at its far end sectioned off by hanging blankets. It was furnished only with the basics — a table, chairs, a Franklin stove and a scratched dresser upon which Kathryn kept china and a few ornaments. While the men took seats at the table, she poured strong coffee into chipped granite mugs and wordlessly passed them around.

Without asking, Bud took a bottle of Old Nick from the dresser and laced each cup with a healthy splash of corn liquor. As he busied himself with tobacco and papers, he asked, 'What do you know about the oil business, Mr. O'Brien?'

'Not a lot.'

'Neither did I, at first,' said Bud. 'I started out drilling salt wells in Alabama. That's how come I got hired to drill my first oil well, in Pennsylvania. I didn't know a thing about it then, but I was a quick study. That first well collapsed fifteen feet down — the ground was pretty much all gravel, see, so there was nothin' to support it. The people who hired me said as how we should give it up as a bad job — but not me. I talked 'em into building a series of pipes ten feet long and five feet wide, that I could hammer into the ground, and they gave us the support we needed to keep drillin'. At forty feet we hit bedrock, and after that I could drill without fear of further collapse. Another forty feet and the oil started coming right up out of the earth.'

He chuckled at the memory, the wheezy chuckle of a man who smoked too much, even as he struck a match and lit his cigarette. He was, O'Brien noticed, very careful to make sure the match was extinguished completely before he threw it into the sardine can that served as an ashtray between them.

'We had to force it out with an old pitcher pump,' he went on, blowing smoke, 'and when we got it out we had to store it in bathtubs!'

Although Don had likely heard the story many times before, he joined in when his father laughed again. Kathryn, however, only picked up some mending and began to sort through it without much interest.

Oblivious to her, Bud continued, 'Well, after that the oil business got into my blood, and it's been there ever since. I was there when they founded Atlantic Petroleum just after the war, and there when Continental Oil an' Transportation came along a decade later. I've worked for Union Oil, South Penn Oil, Vacuum Oil and Standard Oil of New Jersey. I know this business inside out. I worked the first steam-powered rigs, watched the industry damn-near die when Tom Edison invented his incandescent light bulb and all but took away the need for oil and gas. Demand — and price — dropped like a stone then . . . but the business is on the rise again, and this time oil is only gonna get bigger. There are still fortunes to be made from it, Mr. O'Brien — an' where we sit right now we've got what could well turn out to be the biggest field anyone's found to date . . . and I want to be the man to bring it in.'

'So what's your problem?'

'Cards on the table, Mr. O'Brien?' said Don, picking up his mug. 'If we don't strike oil within the next four days, we're finished . . . Congressman Norris and his consortium are out of a small fortune, and — '

' — and my reputation's shot to hell,' Bud finished bitterly. 'Norris can rebuild his fortune. I doubt I can rebuild my reputation, not at my age.'

'What happens four days from now?'

'The lease runs out,' said Temple. 'Or rather, the *sub*-lease.'

'I don't understand.'

'The rancher who owns all the land hereabouts — '

'Graves?'

Temple raised an eyebrow in surprise. 'You've heard of him?'

'I know he's opened up his land to speculation,' said O'Brien.

'What he's done,' Don clarified, 'is lease out the right to develop and exploit the mineral rights under the earth. If the lease runs out before the lessee can accomplish that, the lessor — Graves — gets his land back.'

'Can't you extend the lease?'

'You can, if the lessor is so minded.'

'But Graves isn't?'

'Not so much Graves,' said Temple, 'as Quillan.'

O'Brien frowned. 'Who *is* Quillan, anyway?'

'He's a bastard,' growled Bud.

'Dad!' Don indicated Kathryn with a quick jerk of his chin. 'There's a lady present.'

'Ah, she's heard worse'n that in her time,' Bud replied dismissively.

'I've had some people check him out for me,' Temple cut in. 'He's a dangerous man, O'Brien. A *very* dangerous man. He came over from Ireland about ten years ago, one step ahead of an arrest warrant.'

'What did he do?'

'Apparently he was a member of a revolutionary group called the Irish Republican Brotherhood, whose aim was to end British rule in Ireland.

Among other things, Quillan was responsible for a series of bombings in London that killed a lot of people and made the country too hot for him. He fled to Canada, where the Brotherhood had supporters, but when the Canadian Brotherhood abandoned its plans to attack various British forts and customs posts, he crossed the border into America, hoping to join the Fenians — that's our equivalent of the Irish Republicans.

'Well, he'd left it too late. The Fenians were pretty much finished by then. So he ended up in Abilene, Kansas, playing cards for a living. A whole spate of shooting trouble followed — apparently he didn't take kindly to being called a cheat — and eventually he was posted out of town. Shortly after that he joined the Dodge City Gang. I don't know if you've heard of them — '

'I have.'

'Then you know they were a pretty tough bunch.'

That was an understatement. The Dodge City Gang had been made up of experienced gunmen like Dave Rudabaugh, Dave Mather and Hoodoo Brown. They'd robbed stagecoaches and trains, rustled cattle, and murdered on an industrial scale before they were finally broken up.

'When Graves got out of the ranching business, he fired his foreman and crew,' Temple went on. 'Then, when his subleases started to sell and folks came in from all points to settle a town — even a temporary one like Sunrise — he realized that he needed someone to oversee his interests. He started looking for a hired gun, and somewhere along the line Quillan's name came up. Quillan in turn hired some of his old acquaintances, and they came to Sunrise, supposedly to keep order.'

'But Sunrise has already got a lawman,' said O'Brien. 'I saw him.'

Bud raised a shaggy brow. 'Harry Chamberlain? Hell, Graves hired Chamberlain because Quillan told him to! Quillan's thinking was that, as long as Sunrise has got a lawman, the U.S. Marshal's office'll leave him alone. Was a U.S. Marshal to come in, he'd see exactly what Quillan's up to, and stop him dead in his tracks.'

'And what *is* Quillan up to?'

'Quillan's a man with his eye on the main chance,' Temple explained. 'He's had enough of selling his gun. Now he wants to sit back and make his money an easier way — by going into the oil business for himself.'

'And rustling?' asked O'Brien.

Temple looked blank. 'What about it?'

'I hear tell they've got a rustling problem in these parts as well. I wondered if he was involved in that, too.'

'I wouldn't know. But it wouldn't surprise me. He brought enough men in with him when he first arrived.'

'All right,' said O'Brien. 'Back to this lease business. How does it work, exactly?'

'Graves sells a sub-lease,' explained

Don, 'which effectively lets the investor take all the risks and his wildcatters do all the work. If nothing comes of it by the time the lease expires, the investor can pay again for the right to keep drilling until he strikes oil, or simply cut his losses and call it a day. But the minute it looks as if he might strike oil, Quillan comes up with some fanciful reason why Graves should foreclose on the lease and refuse to allow for an extension. That way all he has to do is take over what's a sure-fire field and reap the profits of some other poor devil's hard work.'

'Can he do that?' asked O'Brien. 'Legally, I mean?'

'Sure he can,' Don confirmed. 'Don't forget, Mr. O'Brien, we're talking about a sub-lease, here. Graves always keeps the top lease for himself. That gives him all the entitlement he needs to claw back a sub-lease if it isn't exploited before it expires.'

'So Graves is up to his neck in it, same as Quillan?'

'No,' said Temple. 'No, I don't think so. But Graves is old and doesn't have any family. He allows himself to be advised by Quillan. If Quillan says the lease shouldn't be renewed, it isn't. But then he buys the lease himself, under an assumed name or a company name, and as far as I can see, Graves is none the wiser.'

'He's done it before,' said Bud. 'We've seen him do it, right here in Sunrise. The minute it looks like one of these fields will come good, Quillan and his bullyboys step in and do whatever they need to obstruct or otherwise delay work until it overruns the deadline. Then they take the lease back, Quillan buys the right to exploit it anew and puts in crews of his own to work it — all nice an' legal . . . and pretty much guaranteed to pay off.'

'If you can prove that, why don't you report it to Chamberlain?'

Temple said, 'In the first place, we can't prove it. Anyone who knows enough to testify against him is too scared to do so. In the second place, you don't know Chamberlain. Once upon a time he was a lawman worth the name. Then he quit his job. Nobody ever knew why, though there was talk that he'd faced down one troublemaker too many, and his nerve had snapped. Anyway, he's an old man now, and just grateful to have a job — which makes him Quillan's man too.'

'And this man Jenner . . . ?' O'Brien began.

Bud stiffened. 'What about Jenner?'

'You two know each other?'

'Know him well enough. He's a good man. Been wildcattin' near as long as me.'

'He's dead,' said Temple. 'Quillan shot him down just before we left town today.'

The blood leeched from Bud's ruddy face and he slowly, carefully butted what was left of his cigarette. 'What happened?' he asked after a moment.

'What always happens,' said Temple. 'Quillan found out that Jenner was

60

about to strike oil, so he had to find a way to delay the strike until after the lease ran out. When all else failed, he decided to set a fire last night that pretty much destroyed Jenner's derrick. When Jenner's brother tried to fight the fire, he was shot dead from ambush. Jenner figured — rightly, in my view — that Quillan was behind it and called him out.'

'Quillan . . . ' Bud breathed, and took a pull direct from the bottle of Old Nick.

'So you're asking me to ride shotgun on this place and make sure Quillan doesn't pull anything similar in the next four days,' said O'Brien.

'Be honest with you, Mr. O'Brien,' said Bud, 'me an' Don are tough as tacks. We can fight our own battles out here. My opinion, bringing in a hired gun's only likely to make things worse. But Norris's got a lot of money tied up in this, much of it on my say-so, so I have to respect his decision.'

'Think you can handle it?' asked

Temple. 'Keep Quillan and his men at bay long enough to let Bud bring this field in?'

'The way you're all talking,' said Kathryn, suddenly breaking her long silence, 'you'd think it's sure to come to a fight. Just maybe it won't. All you have to do is strike oil, and you've done it. This man Quillan can then pay you for what the field's worth, or you can refuse his offer and pay to keep exploiting it yourselves.'

'And you think he'll leave it at that?' asked Don. 'No, Kath, he'll try every trick in the book to delay us, so that we default on the lease. He's already made a start by delaying delivery on the supplies we need, and deliberately sending out wrong or damaged goods. Then he'll have it all . . . and it won't have cost him even a fraction of what this field's worth. Besides, if what Mr. Temple says is right about what happened to Jeff Jenner, he's already living up to his reputation — which means we'll be in for a fight whether we want one or not.'

O'Brien looked at Bud. 'Think you can bring it in on time, Bud?'

'We're down close to four thousand feet,' Bishop replied. 'That's deeper than I ever drilled before. Forget experience — plain common sense tells me it can't be much deeper.'

They watched him, waiting for him to make up his mind.

'Only a fool passes up what he stands to make from this deal,' said Kathryn, and looking him straight in the eye, she added, 'And you don't strike me as a fool, Mr. O'Brien.'

He wasn't. But neither was he reckless. That's why he thought some more about just how fast Quillan had been with his Colts. If it came to shooting between them, he didn't think he stood a chance in hell — not in his present condition, probably not even if he was at full strength. Besides, the memories of his previous beating and recovery — of days spent drifting in and out of consciousness, of the pain he'd endured just to be able to sit up again, then stand up, then begin the long haul back to full fitness — were still fresh.

And yet, like it or not, this was what he did for a living. It was the only way of life he knew, the only way of life that gave him any real measure of satisfaction.

And so he said, very definitely, 'All right, folks — deal me in.'

4

That settled, O'Brien, Temple and Bud went back outside, and at O'Brien's insistence, the wildcatter gave him a quick tour of the lease. He wasn't so much concerned with how the rig worked — he doubted he would ever understand *that* — but he needed to fix the layout of the place in his mind so that he could identify ways to protect and hold it right up to the deadline.

It seemed to him that the most vulnerable part of the entire set-up was the engine house, which contained a chunky steam engine that was about fourteen feet long and shaped like an overturned *L*. Without the steam engine to keep working the drill, Bud was finished — so that made it a prime target for any would-be saboteur.

'All right,' he said, 'let's see about packing dirt up around the sides and across the roof. If Quillan tries to burn it, like he did at Jenner's lease, the dirt might just stop or slow the fire from taking hold.'

'Good idea,' said Temple. 'Do you think we should keep a guard on duty through the night?'

O'Brien nodded. 'How many men has Quillan got?' he asked. 'Do you know?'

'Not for sure,' said the attorney. 'But all the people I've spoken to say he came in ahead of a small army.'

'Well,' said O'Brien, drily, 'as long as it's only a small one.'

He peered up at the derrick, which had been built over something Bud had called a mud pit, through the center of which he was sinking a drill that, surprisingly, was no more than four inches thick.

'How safe is that crow's nest right at the top?' he asked.

'Safe as a mother's lap,' Bud replied instantly. 'Why?'

'It must afford a hell of a view. We'll

have your men take turns up there, keeping watch.'

'Fair enough — if he can stand the noise for any length of time.'

'Tell him to wad up some cloth and plug his ears.'

'All right. What about the perimeter?'

O'Brien was about to reply when the stack of lumber they were passing spat splinters at him.

Temple said, 'What — ?'

The snap of the shot came then, explaining everything.

O'Brien yelled, 'Get down!'

He threw himself behind the lumber, and to hell with his aches and pains. Temple and Bud, meanwhile, bolted for the relatively safety of the Conestoga beside the makeshift corral.

O'Brien yelled, 'Bishop!'

'Here!'

'Throw me my rifle!'

The wildcatter edged along the side of the wagon, then dodged sideways to put the spooked saddle mounts between him and their unseen attacker. Another shot rang out; the piled lumber took another hit, and then they all heard Kathryn, who had stayed in the dugout, yell, 'Don, no!'

Don came out of the dugout with a twelve-gauge Moore & Company shotgun clenched in his oily fists. He paused momentarily, looking for the shooter. Then dirt exploded at his feet, followed quickly by the sound of the shot itself, and he sprinted for cover behind a stack of tarpaulin-covered supplies.

Bud called, 'O'Brien!'

O'Brien turned as the wildcatter threw him his Winchester. Rising up, he caught it, worked the lever, then took off his hat and looked around the lumber, not over it.

'What's happening?' called Temple. 'Wh-who is — ?'

O'Brien saw a covey of quail burst out of a stand of red cedars about two hundred yards away, showing gold against the gray clouds. At the same time, another slug drilled into the piled lumber. The quails' *pit-pit* cry of alarm mixed with the sound of the shot.

He came up, Winchester stock slapped to his shoulder. Allowing for the drop of the bullet over such a distance, he fired, levered, fired, levered and fired again, grouping his shots on the bushwhacker's most likely position. Then he ducked down again just before the lumber took another hit.

The bushwhacker would expect him to return fire again after that, and doubtless be there to blow his head off the moment he showed it. In no hurry to oblige him, O'Brien stayed right where he was, every sense in him strung taut as barbwire.

Behind him the drill kept thumping, the ground beneath him vibrating to every blow.

'M-Mr. O'Brien?' Temple hissed from behind the wagon.

O'Brien ignored him.

Disturbed by the shooting, a crab spider scuttled up and over the top plank of wood. A black and yellow flower-fly briefly hummed around the spent shell-cases next to him before moving on.

Then —

Another bullet cored into the other side of the lumber pile.

This time he *did* come back up, and though visibility in the distant timber was lousy, he spotted their would-be assailant by his light-colored pants as his horse turned and lunged deeper into the cedars.

He put the Winchester's foresight on the retreating figure, led it a little and then squeezed the trigger. By rights, the bushwhacker should have galloped straight into the shot: instead, O'Brien saw bark burst from a tree right beside him, and the bushwhacker kept going.

Again he worked the lever, steadied his aim . . .

. . . then relaxed.

The bushwhacker was gone, lost among the trees and by now too far away to ensure anything like accurate shooting. Neither was there anything to be gained by going in pursuit. They'd meet again: O'Brien would see to it.

Automatically he began to reload the Winchester with .44/.40s he kept in one of the pockets of his wolfskin jacket. As he did so, he decided that the bushwhacker had chosen his spot well. All he'd had to do was set himself up in the cover of those cedars and wait for his targets to show themselves. The only thing that had worked against him was the distance. Two hundred yards, give or take, was about the upper limit for accurate shooting with a long gun.

'It's all right,' he called at last. 'He's gone.'

Cautiously, Temple and the others came out of hiding. The hired men looked edgy. Bud himself swore like a freighter, rarely using the same word twice as he called the bushwhacker all the names he could think of.

Kathryn appeared in front of the dugout and after a moment hurried toward O'Brien, hardly bothering to spare Don a glance. 'Are you all right?' she asked.

'Yes'm.'

'It was you he was after, wasn't it?' she said. 'It was you he kept shooting at.'

Without bothering to reply, he went to his horse, sheathed the Winchester and remounted. As the others watched, he cantered out to the cedars. Although he rode wary, the disturbed quail were even now returning to their nests, and that alone was enough to convince him that their assailant hadn't doubled back to try his luck again.

When he was almost to the trees, he dismounted and left the blood-bay ground-tied. One quick look back over his shoulder to get his bearings, and he went ahead on foot into the cedars.

The earth was spongy in there, and held tracks well. Even a novice could have picked up the churned trail the bushwhacker had left behind him.

He followed the tracks back until he noted a distinctive, rotten-egg smell that told him where the bushwhacker's horse, having been tethered to a low bough, had urinated. He examined the tree briefly, retrieved something wispy from a broken stub of branch, and then doubled back to the tree behind which the bushwhacker himself had hidden, which was nearby.

Here, he went down on one knee and looked around some more. Carefully he picked fallen cedar fronds away from the base of the tree until he found a scattering of brass shell cases, and what he'd been half-expecting to find.

He went back to his horse, remounted and returned to the lease. Everyone gathered around as he rode in.

'What did you find?' asked Temple.

O'Brien held up the butt of a black-paper cigarette, then tossed it aside.

The attorney scowled. 'And that tells us . . . ?'

' . . . enough,' O'Brien replied, dismounting.

'I don't follow you.'

'All I saw of whoever bushwhacked us was the light-colored pants he was wearing,' he explained. 'To me, they

73

looked an awful lot like the nankeen pants Nate Newton was wearing earlier today. The black-paper cigarette butt just about clinches it — Newton was smoking one just like it when Quillan shot Jenner.'

'Newton!'

'I don't know why you're so surprised. It was you told me he'd make a play for me.'

'Well . . . yes, but . . . I mean, a black-paper cigarette? You can't hang a man on that kind of evidence.'

'Maybe not,' said O'Brien. 'But if Newton rides a bay and white paint horse, that'll settle it.'

'How so?'

'Because I also spotted this caught on a branch where the bushwhacker tied his mount.'

He held out a small tuft of hair, mixing white strands with reddish-brown.

Temple looked doubtful. 'I'd urge you to make absolutely sure of this before you go making any trouble,' he advised. 'You insulted him, certainly . . . but would he honestly take a shot at you just for that?'

'Maybe he wasn't aiming just at me. Maybe Quillan ordered him to throw a scare into all of us.'

Bud growled. 'You got a point there. There's nothin' that skinny cur wouldn't do for Quillan.' He pulled his derby forward a little on his gray hair. 'Well, I'll fix his wagon — '

'You'll stay here, keep your eyes open and keep that drill working,' O'Brien replied grimly. 'Now that I'm on the payroll, settling accounts is *my* job.'

★   ★   ★

It was late afternoon by the time they got back to Sunrise. They put their horses up at the livery where Temple had rented his sorrel, and because it was just across the street from The Christmas Tree, O'Brien checked the stalls for a bay and white horse.

He found one in an end stall.

The stable hand, a young man in rolled shirtsleeves, watched him curiously. 'You got a problem there, mister?' he called.

'Just wondered who the horse belongs to,' O'Brien replied.

'That's Nate Newton's cayuse,' the stable hand said, as if the answer should be obvious.

O'Brien traded a brief glance with Temple. 'Thought it might be. Take it Nate's been out on him this afternoon?'

'Yessir. Got back not more'n thirty minutes ago.'

O'Brien came back along the aisle and paid for the care of his horse. 'Thanks.'

Outside, they stood for a moment, watching the crowds and listening to the remorseless *thump . . . thump . . . thump* coming from the oil field to the north.

'What, ah . . . now?' Temple asked apprehensively.

'I go buy myself a drink,' said O'Brien.

'At The Christmas Tree, I suppose?'

'At The Christmas Tree,' O'Brien confirmed.

'You do know, of course, that's exactly what Newton expects you to do. He'll be ready and waiting. And bracing him on his own ground, where he's got the rest of Quillan's hired guns to back him . . . you're likely to get yourself killed. Worse than that, you're likely to get me killed alongside you. And I want no part of that. Aside from my obligations to Senator Norris, I have a fiancée waiting for me back home in Maryland.'

'Then go back to your hotel,' said O'Brien. 'There's no call for you to get involved in this, anyway.'

'I'm already involved.'

'Just go back to your hotel,' O'Brien repeated. 'I'll come up and see you again before I head back to the lease.'

He turned, crossed the street, went up toward the saloon and pushed through the batwings.

Butter-colored light cast by two candle wheel chandeliers showed him the usual set-up — a spacious barroom with a duckboard floor, a scattering of tables and chairs, some men playing billiards, others trying their luck with Faro, poker or three-card monte. A big man in white shirt and black pants sat on a high chair just to one side of the doorway, a Purdey shotgun across his lap. A staircase to the right led to a gallery and cribs above. Beside the staircase, a fat woman with blonde hair and heavy makeup played a Bechstein piano passably well. A heavy pall of cigar and cigarette smoke floated lazily around the tin ceiling.

He headed for the plank-and-barrel counter that ran the length of the back wall, where two bartenders in sleeve garters were dispensing cheer as fast as they could. Another seemingly casual glance around finally showed him a back door and, beside it, a baize-topped table set well back in a shadowed corner, at which Hugh Quillan was playing poker with Nate Newton and another man — bulky, with red hair and a cowhorn mustache of the same distinctive color.

As Quillan looked up and spotted him, O'Brien turned his attention back to the bar, where he found space and ordered a whiskey.

'Make that two,' said Temple, shouldering in beside him.

O'Brien eyed him askance. 'I thought you were all set for an early night.'

'Let's just say that curiosity got the better of my survival instincts,' Temple returned dourly. He inspected their surroundings with clear distaste and muttered, 'Now I know how David must've felt.'

'Come again?'

'Don't you know your scripture?'

'Not much call for scripture in my line.'

'Well, I refer you to Samuel, 17:35. A lion stole one of David's sheep, and he went after it, caught it by its beard and killed it.'

'What's that got to do with anything?'

'I think you're up to more than just

'settling accounts', Mr. O'Brien. It might be interesting to see what it is — provided I live long enough.'

Their drinks came and Temple examined the cloudy whiskey with a grimace.

'Why is this place called The Christmas Tree, anyway?' asked O'Brien.

'It's a wildcatting term,' Temple replied. 'What else would it be in a town like this? It's the spot where they place all the control valves, pressure gauges and chokes to control the flow of oil once it's been struck.' He raised his glass in toast and said, ironically, 'To your continued good health. And mine.'

Over the sounds of men drinking, glasses clinking and the lady pianist playing 'The Tune the Old Cow Died On', O'Brien sensed a sudden lowering of voices, a tailing-off of conversation, and so was in no way surprised when someone pushed in on his other side and tapped him hard on one shoulder.

Turning, he found himself looking at Nate Newton.

Newton said, 'You're O'Brien?'

O'Brien nodded.

'I hear you been bad-mouthin' me.'

Up close, Newton was a stringbean of a man, pared down to the bone, and through the languorous gauze of smoke that curled upward from the black-paper cigarette tucked into the corner of his whisker-darkened mouth, his black eyes looked somehow haunted and restless. He was too jumpy for the kind of bullyboy work he did, but there was good money to be made from it, and that made it hard to walk away from.

'What did I say?' O'Brien asked innocently.

'You said I was a back-shooter.'

The buzz of conversation had faded almost entirely now, and several nearby drinkers shifted a little, to get out of the line of fire if it should come to shooting. The big man on the high chair started to bring his shotgun up but suddenly stopped, and O'Brien knew that Quillan had gestured that he should sit this one out.

'Uh-huh,' O'Brien replied with a shake of the head. 'You heard wrong, Nate. I said there was nothing you wouldn't do for money. How you take that's your affair.'

Newton cocked his head. 'You're not tryin' awful hard to dodge a fight, are you?'

'With you? I'm not trying at all.'

Newton grinned coolly. 'I'm glad to hear you say that.'

'Why — because it gives you the chance to finish what you started this afternoon?'

O'Brien was looking him straight in the eye when he said it, and Newton didn't disappoint. His eyes — almost constantly on the move anyway — quickly fell away from O'Brien's, then came back.

'What's that supposed to mean?'

'Come on, Nate, let's not play games. It's been a long day, and I get real fractious when someone tries to shoot me from ambush.'

'I don't claim to know what you're

yammerin' about,' said Newton, 'but let's go outside and settle this thing like men.'

'In the street?' asked O'Brien. 'A mite crowded, wouldn't you say?'

'The yard out back.'

'And what if I say no?'

'Then you can apologize for what you called me . . . and everyone here'll see you for the gizzard-eatin' coward you are.'

An apprehensive rustle went through the onlookers.

'I've got a better idea,' said O'Brien. 'Let's settle it right here.'

Newton spat his cigarette out. 'Outside,' he said again. 'More room out there.'

'Here,' insisted O'Brien. 'Now.'

Sweat tickled Newton's forehead, and when he blinked it was more like a flinch. 'I don't aim to put any o' these other folks at risk,' he said piously.

'They won't be at risk,' O'Brien assured him. 'Because this time I'll hit what I aim at.'

'Outside,' Newton said, sounding desperate now.

'No,' O'Brien said, firmer. 'Because when I kill you, Nate, it'll be straight-up, not set up.'

Newton scowled. 'What the hell's that suppo — '

O'Brien's right fist came out of nowhere and slammed hard against Newton's jaw. Newton's eyes rolled up and he slumped against the bar. He clung there for a few seconds, then relaxed, dropping into a muscle-stiff heap at O'Brien's feet.

'Drink up,' O'Brien told Temple, his voice sounding loud in the shocked silence.

Still stunned by what had happened, Temple did as he was told, then set his glass down and turned toward the batwings until O'Brien put a hand on his arm.

'Now what?' asked the attorney.

'Humor me,' said O'Brien.

Instead of heading for the exit, he walked slowly across the bar toward the table at which Quillan had been playing cards. The crowd opened up before him, and after a slight hesitation, Temple followed at his heels.

Quillan, all alone now, watched him come, a merry light playing in his green eyes. It seemed that nothing could faze him; he really did believe he could handle anything that came his way.

O'Brien came to a halt and looked down at him.

'Y'know,' Quillan said conversationally, 'you're not the most sociable man I ever met.'

'Must be something about getting shot at that rubs me the wrong way.'

'Ah, I wouldn't know about that. Anyway, any trouble you've got with Nate is your business. Don't drag me into it.'

'Then don't send him out with orders to shoot me.'

Quillan's expression relaxed into one of pure innocence. 'I'm sure I don't know what ye mean . . . mack.'

'That's funny,' said O'Brien, 'because

'I'm sure you do.'

'Have a care,' said Quillan. 'I don't take kindly to bein' called a liar.'

'Then fight your own battles in future,' said O'Brien, 'instead of ordering it done.'

Quillan eyed him with fresh interest. 'Fancy your chances, do ye?'

'One way to find out.'

Quillan thought about it, but not for long. A gunfight in here, right now, would be bad for business — especially if any of his customers were caught in the overspill. Besides which, O'Brien was standing — perfectly balanced, too, the Irishman noted with a professional's eye for such things — while he was seated, and at a disadvantage if it came to gunplay.

'Maybe you're right,' he allowed at length. 'But this is neither the time nor the place. So do yourself a favor — ride on.'

'I'll go when I'm good and ready,' said O'Brien. 'Meantime, you can do *me* a favor.'

Quillan made a magnanimous gesture with one hand. 'Name it.'

'See us back to the hotel, will you? Just to make sure nothing *else* happens to me or Temple today.'

Aware that all eyes were on him, Quillan offered a hearty laugh, even though his eyes remained frosty. 'You tellin' me you can't cross the street by yerself?'

'I'm telling you that three men were sitting here when I came in. Now there's only you. I know what happened to Newton. I don't know for sure what happened to the other one, the redhead . . . but I can guess.' His eyes flickered briefly toward the back door. 'He's been out there in the yard, waiting for Newton to get me out there so he can gun me down from the shadows.'

'Ye got quite an imagination, haven't ye?'

'Why else would Newton be so keen to get me out there?'

'Now, I'm sure you've got it all wrong,' Quillan said mildly.

'You're crossing that street with us, anyway,' said O'Brien. 'Because if your man out there takes it into his head to go around front and try shooting at us when we leave, I'll be taking you with us.'

Quillan's eyelids dropped ever so slightly. 'Get out of here,' he said.

'Not without you.'

Slowly, keeping his hands well away from his sides, the Irishman stood up. 'Well, come along, then,' he said in that usual hearty manner of his. 'If it'll soothe yer nerves any.'

He picked up his hat as he came around the table and slowly put it on. O'Brien watched him all the time, just in case. But Quillan only swaggered to the batwings, with O'Brien and Temple following behind. There, O'Brien came alongside him, and put his left arm around Quillan's shoulders.

'Come on, then, pard,' he said, and they went out onto the boardwalk together, like the best of friends.

Sunrise still hadn't slowed down any.

Wagons rattled past, men scurried back and forth. O'Brien's eyes were everywhere at once, but when nothing happened immediately, he said again, 'Come on.'

As they crossed the street, Quillan said in an undertone, 'Ye know I'm goin' to kill ye, don't ye?'

'I know you're going to try.'

'We could save all this unpleasantness, ye know,' Quillan continued. 'All ye got to do is come an' work for me — or get the hell out of Sunrise, an' no harm done.'

'I'll stick around,' said O'Brien. 'And I've already got a job.'

'The Bishop well,' said Quillan.

'The Bishop well,' O'Brien confirmed. 'And you better pray that nothing happens to stop Bishop bringing that well in on time, Quillan, because if it does, if anything at all holds him back . . . I'll be holding you responsible.'

Quillan made a tutting sound. 'Ah, O'Brien,' he said with mock regret. 'Ye just went an' sealed your fate for good. Ye see, if there's one thing I can't abide, it's a man who threatens me.'

'*You* just threatened *me*,' O'Brien reminded him. 'I reckon that makes us even.'

'All right,' Quillan allowed. 'We're even. But tomorrow, we start afresh, the pair of us.' He indicated the hotel with a casual jut of his rugged, dimpled jaw. 'Well, will you look at that? You made it across the street in one piece after all. Can I go now?'

'Sure.'

'An' no fear of gettin' a bullet the minute I turn me back?'

'I'll tell you what I told Newton,' O'Brien replied. 'When I kill you, it'll be straight up.'

Quillan's mouth smiled. His eyes didn't.

'I'm goin' to enjoy watchin' you squirm before ye die,' he said. 'They do that, ye know, men who've been gut-shot. They squirm, just like man-size worms.'

'Carry on like that,' O'Brien said easily, 'you'll give me nightmares.'

Quillan's smile became a chuckle. 'Ye know, in spite of everything, I like you, O'Brien. You've got guts. Too bad I have to spill 'em. But you know how it is. This is a tough town. A man has to be tough to make his way in it.'

He turned away, stopped, turned back.

'As we say back in the old country,' he added pleasantly, 'tranquil sleep.'

★   ★   ★

The minute they entered the hotel and Temple saw that the clerk was nowhere around, he turned to O'Brien and said, 'So that's why we went to The Christmas Tree — to declare war!'

'The war's already been declared,' O'Brien reminded him. 'What I did was set an example.'

'What's that supposed to mean?'

'Right now,' O'Brien explained patiently, 'Quillan's got this town buffaloed. No one dares stand up to him because they know they'll get what Jenner got this morning. Well, maybe I've just shown them that he's not going to have it all his own way. Could be that'll encourage the rest to stand up to him.'

'You've got it the wrong way around,' said Temple. 'It's Quillan who'll be using *you* as an example. He's got to — you haven't left him any choice.'

'I've given him as much choice as he gave Jenner.'

'He'll be back.'

'He'd be back anyway. But now there's no doubt about it — he knows we're going to fight him every step of the way. It might not make him think twice for long . . . but maybe it'll buy us some time before he makes his next move.'

Temple looked at him as if he were seeing him for the first time. 'You've got it all worked out, haven't you?' he said.

'No. But it's always been my experience that the more you confound the other feller, the more apt he is to make a mistake. He does that, he gives us an edge.'

Temple released a breath. 'Congressman Norris pays my wages, so I have to respect his wishes, but . . . '

'But . . . ?'

'But if Quillan plays any rougher than he already has, and someone gets hurt because of it, I'm holding *you* responsible, O'Brien. You've pushed him, and now he'll start pushing back.'

O'Brien gave him a grim smile. 'I'll be waiting for him,' he said softly.

5

O'Brien was up and around long before dawn the next morning. They started work early out at the Bishop well, and even before the sun began to show, the steam engine growled to life amidst much yelling of orders and acknowledgements. The cables started to pump and snap, and then, screechingly at first, the drill began to rise and fall in its resin pipe socket, and the cot beneath him shook to the sound.

He rolled out, stripped to the waist, then crossed over to the trough, where he filled a pan with cold water, lathered up and shaved.

Halfway through the shave Kathryn appeared in the dugout doorway and watched him openly for a few minutes before calling, 'Can I get you some breakfast?'

He shook his head and finished

toweling off. 'Maybe later, thanks all the same.'

He returned to the wall tent to finish dressing.

By the time he'd returned to the well the previous evening, the Bishops had carried out his orders for the protection of the engine house, and one of the hired men had been posted at the top of the derrick, rifle in hands and ears crudely plugged against the noise, to keep watch on their surroundings. Briefly, while Kathryn ladled a tasteless beef stew onto enamel plates, he'd told them all what had happened in town, at the end of which Bud nodded approvingly.

'That's it,' he said. 'Let the bastard know just what we think of him, an' tell him to do his worst!'

'And that's just what he *will* do,' Don predicted.

'Well, I agree with Bud,' said Kathryn, giving O'Brien an approving glance. 'It's about time someone stood up to that Irishman.'

After supper, O'Brien had stood first watch. He didn't think Quillan would make another move against them so soon, but maybe that's what Quillan would want them to think. He was relieved at midnight by a taciturn wildcatter named Baker, and bedded down in the wall tent. The remainder of the night passed quietly.

A little after seven o'clock the man standing watch at the top of the derrick yelled a warning. But O'Brien had already seen the single rider coming in from the direction of Sunrise astride a bay roan. As he crossed the lease to meet the newcomer, Bud Bishop jumped down from the engine house and joined him.

'That's Harry Chamberlain,' he muttered, pushing his derby hat back off his lined forehead. 'What the hell does he want?'

When the lawman was close enough, O'Brien nodded a greeting and said, 'Morning, Marshal.'

Up close, Chamberlain was a cadaverous man of medium height in a gray suit with a silver star pinned to the lapel. He was in his early sixties and looked it. The tired, pale face beneath his gray Stetson was long and clean-shaven, with a straight nose, flared nostrils and a sober mouth. But it was his very blue eyes that dominated his face: they were almost startling in their sadness.

Returning the scrutiny, Chamberlain snapped, 'You answer to the name of O'Brien?'

'Uh-huh.'

'Then you're under arrest. Best you come peaceable.'

'What's he supposed to have done?' asked Kathryn, hurrying over to join them.

'Assaulted Nate Newton at The Christmas Tree last night.'

'You call that assault — ?' began Bud.

'Well, that's what Newton's callin' it, and he's got a saloon full of witnesses to back him up.'

'Quillan's cronies,' said Bud.

'That's not for me to say,' said

Chamberlain. 'Thing is, a complaint's been filed, an' I'm duty-bound to investigate it.'

'Of course you are,' said the wildcatter. ''Cause you're Quillan's man, too.'

Chamberlain squared his shoulders. 'Because I'm the law.'

'Don't hand me that,' Bud said scathingly. 'Everyone knows Quillan brought you in before the U.S. Marshal's office could send out a *real* lawman.'

The comment hit Chamberlain like a slap, but he bit down the response he intended to make and said instead, 'You need to come in to my office and answer these charges, O'Brien. You comin' peaceable or not?'

O'Brien didn't reply at once. He was wondering if this was some kind of trap — that instead of riding back to town he'd be riding straight into an ambush. He looked up at the elderly marshal, trying to read his expression. The first thing that struck him was that Chamberlain didn't handle himself like a man who'd lost his nerve. Neither did he have the look of a Judas goat, a man who would set up another.

He could only hope he was right about that.

'I'll come with you,' he replied after a moment, seeing little real alternative. 'But only so that I can put my side of it on record, and keep everything official. Then you can go back to Newton and ask him if he still wants to make something out of it.'

Chamberlain eyed him curiously. 'This is a serious charge,' he said. 'You know that, right?'

'I know it. But it's only serious if Newton decides to push it. He does that, you've got no choice but to throw me in jail. You do that, I have to stand trial. Now, I don't know how you're fixed for a circuit judge in these parts, but I do know that Jim Temple's a lawyer, and he knows some important people. He can probably get a judge out here in less time that it takes dust to settle. And when he gets here, he's going to find out what Quillan's up to and call in the federal law. You put it that way to Newton, I've got a feeling he'll drop the charges.'

Chamberlain wasn't entirely able to mask the smile that played fleetingly at his mouth. 'I got a feeling you're right,' he replied. 'All right — get your horse and let's go.'

A few minutes later they were headed back to town, O'Brien riding wary and still trying to gauge whether or not Chamberlain's real purpose here today had been to lead him into a trap.

'You do know,' he said at last, 'if we should run into any trouble on the way back to town, you'll be the first man to die.'

Chamberlain threw him a glance. 'Is that a fact?'

'Just so you know, Marshal.'

'Well, just so *you* know,' said Chamberlain, 'if anyone was to try anythin' 'tween here an' Sunrise, they'd be interferin' with due process . . . in which case I'd cloud up and rain all over 'em.'

O'Brien considered that. If Chamberlain was a liar, he was the best O'Brien had seen.

'Don't think I swallowed Newton's story for a second,' the lawman continued. 'I don't know you, O'Brien, but I've heard of you. Figured right off you must have had a reason for knockin' him cold.'

'I did,' O'Brien said. 'Want to hear it?'

'Sure. It'll pass the ride. Then you can write it all down in a statement and sign it.'

O'Brien recounted the events of the previous afternoon, when someone had shot at them all from hiding.

'That still doesn't give you the right to assault Newton,' Chamberlain said when he was finished. 'You didn't really get a good look at him. It could have been anyone.'

'It was him, all right.'

'Maybe it was. But your evidence'd never stand up in court.'

'Probably not. But it was good

enough for me. As for assaulting him, it was knock him out or kill him.'

'How'd you figger that?'

'When he braced me, he made it seem like he was pushing for a fight. What he really wanted was to get me out into that yard behind The Christmas Tree, where one of his buddies could back-shoot me.'

'If that's right,' Chamberlain said after a moment, 'and knowing Newton, I'll allow it's a possibility, why does he want you dead?'

'It's not so much him as Quillan.'

'All right — why does Quillan want you dead?'

'Are you telling me you really don't know?'

'I can work it out,' Chamberlain replied. 'But why don't you save me the exercise?'

'The Bishop well,' said O'Brien.

'Talk is, that one's gonna be a gusher.'

'Then you can guess why Quillan wants it.'

'So what makes you such a threat?'

'Because I've been hired to make it just as hard as I can for him to get his hands on it.'

'I'll confess, it hangs together,' said the lawman.

'But your hands are tied, is that what you're going to tell me?'

'Quillan hired me, right enough,' said the marshal. 'But Bud Bishop back there, he got it wrong. I'm not Quillan's man. I work for the law.'

'Then you're kidding yourself, Marshal. Because from what I hear, Quillan's the only law in this town.'

Chamberlain wasn't prepared to argue that. Instead, echoing Temple, he said, 'You're gonna start a damn war here, ain't you?'

'There's no need for that — if you warn Quillan off the way you're trying to warn me off.'

'Quillan hasn't broken any laws.'

'What about Jeff Jenner?'

'I'll admit, that was a sad affair. But as I understand it, a fire broke out in

Jenner's storage shed, and he blamed Quillan — just like you, with not a shred of evidence.'

'And his brother? The one who was shot dead when he tried to put the fire out?'

Chamberlain's lips compressed. 'You only got into town yesterday,' he noted. 'You don't know what it was like.'

'So educate me.'

'Jenner convinced himself that all of his problems had been caused by Quillan. He just couldn't prove it. So he armed his men and gave 'em orders to shoot first when it came to defending the well.'

'You're saying it was Jenner's own men who killed his brother?'

'Who's to say it wasn't? The fire caught fast, got out of control. Everyone was panicking, chasing around. Mistakes happen.'

'Very convenient for Quillan.'

'You think I don't know that?' Chamberlain flared. 'But I'm a lawman, O'Brien. I work according to the law. If you bring me hard evidence, I'll tackle him. You bring me gossip, there's not a damn thing I can do for you.'

O'Brien held his silence. But he sensed that Chamberlain meant what he said, and if he did . . . well, maybe he wasn't Quillan's man, after all. Maybe Quillan had heard the same rumors as everyone else and convinced himself he was buying a puppet lawman. If that was the case, and push ever came to shove, that might just prove to be the Irishman's undoing.

Still . . .

'I've heard of you, too,' he said carefully.

Chamberlain smiled sourly at that. 'I can imagine what you've heard. Same as everyone else, I 'spect.'

'I hear you used to be a hell of a lawman.'

'It's that *used to be* part I don't like.'

The town appeared up ahead, an ugly blot on a similarly ugly, dead-grass plain, and O'Brien's attention was once again drawn to Sunrise's miserable little cemetery. A few men were gathered around two fresh graves, while the chubby little Presbyterian preacher spoke a few words over a pair of cheap coffins. O'Brien recognized one of the mourners as the lanky negro who'd tried to restrain Jenner the day before.

'The Jenners,' muttered Chamberlain, taking off his hat.

O'Brien did likewise.

They pushed on then, and though the air was filled with the metronomic hammering of drill bits coming from the north, the town itself was still reasonably quiet. As they passed *The Christmas Tree*, O'Brien spotted Hugh Quillan watching them from just inside the saloon doorway, his arms resting on the curved tops of the ornate batwings. Quillan's teeth flashed in a grin and he threw O'Brien a jaunty little salute, which O'Brien ignored. He didn't think the Irishman would pick a fight with him right now, but he wasn't so sure about Newton. And not seeing Newton around made him feel itchy.

'Come on,' said Chamberlain.

They reached the law office, swung down and tied up at the rack out front. Then Chamberlain gestured that O'Brien should precede him inside. The square, squat, sturdy single room behind the thick pine door was furnished with a desk, a couple of chairs, a file cabinet and an empty rifle rack. The room was separated down the middle by a wall of iron bars, so that the back half served as a communal cell that was empty right then.

The black water spaniel O'Brien had seen beside the marshal the day before was waiting for him when he came in. The dog jumped down off the marshal's old captain's chair, padded over, wagged his tail and the lawman scratched at his sleek fur.

'Nice dog,' said O'Brien, bending to pet the animal as it sniffed at the cuffs of his corduroy pants.

'Eddie, here?' said Chamberlain. 'He was here when I arrived. Took a shine to me, an' been around ever since. Take a chair, O'Brien. You can write, I guess?'

'I can.'

'Well, here you go,' said Chamberlain, producing some paper from a drawer on the business side of the desk and gesturing to the pen in the inkwell. 'Get to it. Everything you just told me.'

As patiently as he could, O'Brien wrote out the events of the previous day as he saw them, then signed the statement and pushed the single sheet back across the desk.

'Let's have a look here,' said Chamberlain, holding it close to his face so that he could read it by the light of the single, barred window. 'Damn eyesight,' he muttered. 'Had a pair of spectacles once, but I sat on 'em.'

He labored over the statement a moment more, then finally nodded as if satisfied.

'All right,' he said. 'I'll go hunt up Newton and see if he wants to stand by his complaint. In the meantime . . . '

His sad eyes indicated the cell, and

O'Brien's manner immediately cooled. 'You're not locking me up, Chamberlain,' he said softly.

'Is that a fact?' asked the marshal. 'You'd better believe it.'

'Then what's to stop you from walkin' right out the minute my back's turned?'

'Two things,' O'Brien replied. 'One — I'll give you my word on it, which ought to be enough by itself.'

'And if it isn't?'

O'Brien gestured to the dog. 'You can always put me in the custody of Eddie, here.'

Chamberlain scowled, at first thinking that O'Brien was poking fun at him. Then he realized his mistake, saw that O'Brien was actually trying to lighten the moment, and once again he gave that rare little half-smile. Deadpan, he pointed a gnarled finger at the dog. 'Eddie,' he said, 'you make sure this here miscreant don't make a break for it while I'm gone, you hear?'

The spaniel wagged his tail.

At the door, the marshal swung back and said, 'You hungry?'

Realizing that he was indeed, O'Brien nodded.

'Well, there's no reason why we shouldn't do this thing civilized,' said Chamberlain. 'I'll order a couple breakfasts from Mamie's on my way up to The Christmas Tree, pick 'em up on the way back. Meantime, there's coffee in the pot. Help yourself.'

'Thanks.'

O'Brien sat for a while after the door closed behind the lawman, still wondering if Chamberlain had been ordered to gain his trust, make him drop his guard and give Quillan and Newton the chance they needed to punch his ticket. Though it was possible, it didn't seem likely.

A half-hour dragged by. Somehow it seemed much longer. Having accepted the job to protect the Bishop well, O'Brien wanted to get on with it. He stood up, looked through the window. Behind him, Eddie wagged his tail. On the other side of the smudged glass, Main Street was now full of life.

At last O'Brien heard boots on the walk outside and a moment later the door opened and the marshal stamped back inside, carrying a covered tray.

'Couldn't find Newton,' he reported. 'Quillan said he was out on some errand or other. So I showed him your statement and suggested that Newton would be wise to let the matter drop.'

'What did Quillan say to that?' asked O'Brien, as Chamberlain set down the tray and uncovered two bone china plates stacked high with steak, eggs, biscuits and gravy.

'He allowed as how that was a sagacious notion. That was the word he used — *sagacious*. Said he'd put it to Newton next time he saw him, and then send someone down with his decision.'

'So I still can't leave?'

'Not until Newton withdraws his complaint.' Chamberlain helped himself to cutlery and said, 'Dig in.'

O'Brien didn't need telling twice.

But as good as the food was, and as seemingly genial the company, the restlessness in him persisted.

'What's ailin' you?' the lawman asked after a while.

'I was just wondering why Newton brought charges against me in the first place.'

'Who knows with a grudge-toter like that?' Chamberlain replied, picking a scrap of food from his teeth. 'Pure cussedness, most like.'

'Maybe. Or . . . '

'Or what?'

'To keep me here in town, instead of out at the well, where I *should* be.'

'What would he have to gain by that?'

Before O'Brien could reply, the door opened and Jim Temple came inside. The attorney took one look at the scene before him and shook his head in wonderment. 'And here's me thinking they were keeping you on a diet of bread and water,' he said.

'Help yourself to coffee, Temple,' invited Chamberlain, stifling a belch.

'We're just waitin' for Newton to make up his mind whether or not he wants to pursue his complaint.'

'What complaint?' asked Temple. 'All I know is what the clerk down at the Sunflower just told me — that he saw you two riding past the hotel, and that *you*, O'Brien, had the look of a prisoner about you.'

O'Brien gave him the shortened version of events, at the end of which Temple dug out and consulted his Waltham pocket watch. The water spaniel looked up at him, eyes bright. 'He's taking his time, isn't he?'

O'Brien pushed the empty plate away. 'That's what I was thinking. Marshal — '

'Have a little patience,' said Chamberlain, adding, 'Try leavin' now an' I'll sic Eddie on you.'

O'Brien smiled, but his uneasiness didn't just persist, it grew. 'Jim,' he said at last. 'Do me a favor. Go up to The Christmas Tree and see what's keeping Newton?'

Temple nodded. 'All ri — '

But just then there was a knock at the door, and a boy of about twelve came inside. 'Message for you, Marshal,' he said, and handed over a piece of paper.

Chamberlain took it, unfolded it, read it, then said, 'Thanks, Charlie.' After the boy was gone, he threw the paper on the desk. 'From Newton. Says he's withdrawing his complaint.'

'About time!' breathed Temple.

O'Brien got to his feet and scratched the dog's head one last time. 'Be seeing you, then, Marshal. Thanks for the breakfast.'

'Welcome,' replied Chamberlain. 'But I'll tell you again what I told Quillan, when I saw him. I don't want a war here, and that I'll jail the first man who tries to start one.'

'How'd he take that?'

'It didn't exactly make me his favorite person. But I didn't take this job to make friends.'

O'Brien studied him for a long moment, again decided Chamberlain was talking straight-arrow. 'Maybe he got you all wrong, Marshal,' he said after a moment, and then glanced meaningfully at Temple. 'Maybe a lot of people have. But war's coming, whether you want it or not. Quillan'll see to it. And when it does, you're going to have to choose sides. I hope you choose the right one.'

'Yours?' asked Chamberlain, raising one eyebrow.

O'Brien shrugged. 'There's always room for a good man on the right side.'

Outside, he said to Temple, 'Ever get the feeling you've been had?'

'How do you mean?'

'I don't know, yet,' he replied, collecting his mount from the rack. 'Come on, let's rent you a horse and go find out.'

★　★　★

Quillan was still watching from the saloon doorway as they rode by. His smile said he was in rare good humor as they came level with him.

O'Brien drew rein and called down, 'Newton in there?'

'He is, indeed,' Quillan replied affably.

'Then tell him to come out here where I can see him.'

Quillan shrugged and called over his shoulder, 'Nate.'

A few seconds passed and then Newton slouched out of the shadows to lounge beside him. The side of his face sported an impressive bruise, and when he spoke, his voice was distorted by the swelling that went with it. 'Come to thank me for not pressin' charges?' he asked.

'Nope,' O'Brien replied flatly. 'I just like bushwhackers where I can see 'em, is all.' His eyes seemed to drill right into Newton. 'Don't get any notions about trying that stunt again, Nate. And you, Quillan — you send anyone else after us, and I'll be coming right after you.'

'That's the way it'll be,' Quillan said with a grin. 'Just ye an' me.'

'Well, you've been told. Be right . . . sagacious . . . if you stay told.'

He turned his horse and rode on, Temple at his side. The attorney matched him all the way out to the Bishop well.

★   ★   ★

O'Brien knew something was wrong long before they passed the poisoned waterhole, went over the timbered rise and across the prairie toward the derrick. After a while, Temple noticed it as well.

'I can't hear any sound from the lease,' he said.

'Nor can I,' said O'Brien, his earlier unease seemingly justified. 'Come on.'

They went over the hill and down toward the well. The place was silent, and apparently deserted. As they closed on it, O'Brien's eyes were everywhere at once, his belly tight with apprehension as he wondered what they would find waiting for them and how it would change the situation.

When they were still about a hundred yards away, the dugout door opened and Bud, Don and Kathryn came out into the overcast. As they rode in, Temple called, 'What's wrong? Where is everyone?'

'Gone,' Don supplied bitterly. 'Nate Newton came out just after O'Brien here left with Marshal Chamberlain. Said there was plenty work back in town since Jenner's well'd been taken over by some mysterious 'new leasee' and offered 'em twice what they're earning here. Good money and none of the risks they run by sticking with us. They'd've been fools *not* to take it.'

O'Brien looked up at the still, silent derrick and thought grimly, *So that was it. Keep me tied up in town while Newton came out here bold as brass and stole Bishop's workforce right out from under him.* He wondered fleetingly if Chamberlain had been part of the plan. He didn't want to think so. He liked Chamberlain, what little he knew of him, and didn't want to have to meet him through gunsmoke if he could help it.

'I figured we could rely on 'em,' Bud said. 'My mistake. The days when a man gave you his word and his hand, they've gone.' His eyes found those of O'Brien. 'Without a decent crew, there's no way we're gonna bring this well in by ourselves.'

'Can't you try hiring some more men in Sunrise?'

'I doubt that Quillan'd make it that easy for us,' said Bud, spitting to one side. 'You can bet he's already put the word out — we're poison in that town.'

'Can we help?' asked Temple.

'This is no job for a greenhorn. You're like to get yourselves killed, you do the wrong thing at the wrong time.'

'Well, we can't just give up,' said Temple. 'You've taken good money, Bud, and plenty of it — '

Bud turned on him, temper rising. 'Then you tell me where I can get a crew that's not scared to go up against Quillan!'

O'Brien said, 'I'll tell you where, Bud. I'll tell you exactly where!'

6

'Jenner's old crew?' snapped Bud.

They'd gone back into the dugout to drink coffee and hold what amounted to a council of war. Now, having rolled and lit himself a cigarette, Bud blew smoke at the low ceiling and shook his head.

'They'll never go for it,' he decided. 'They've seen first-hand just how rough Quillan plays. I doubt they'd want any part of goin' against him again.'

'Surely it's worth asking them?' argued Kathryn. 'I mean, they'll be looking for jobs elsewhere, now that Newton's taken our men to work Jenner's lease.'

'And they were willing to fight before,' O'Brien reminded the little wild-catter. 'Jenner gave them rifles and they did the best they could against whoever fired their storage shed.'

'Putting it that way,' said Don, 'we've got nothing to lose by asking 'em.'

'Johnny Organ might consider it, I guess,' mused Bud.

Temple frowned. 'Who's he?'

'Jenner's man. Big black feller.'

'He was there this morning, when they buried Jenner and his brother.'

'But I can't speak for the others,' Bud continued. 'They say no, we're still dead in the water.'

'And if they say yes,' said O'Brien, '*you're* back in business.'

Bud drew on his cigarette. 'Kath,' he muttered, 'pass me that bottle.'

She did as he asked and he splashed Old Nick into his coffee before offering it around. 'All right,' he decided after a while. 'It beats sittin' around here, admittin' defeat. I'll ride into Sunrise and see if I can find 'em. If Johnny Organ goes for it, one or more of the others might be tempted to join him.'

'I'll go with you,' said O'Brien.

Bud threw him a scowl. 'Think I need a nursemaid?'

'I think you might need a body-guard,' O'Brien corrected him. 'If Quillan sees you in town, alone . . . well, there's no telling what he might try, if he thinks it'll stop you from drilling.'

'Do to me what he did to the Jenners, you mean?'

'Not necessarily. But an 'accident' could leave you badly injured. Too bad to keep drilling.'

'There's still Don,' Bud reminded him.

Before she could stop herself, Kathryn snorted and said, 'Don's not *you*.'

An awkward silence filled the dugout.

'Thanks,' Don said sourly.

'I didn't mean it the way it came out,' she said irritably. 'Look, are we going to get this well back up and running or not?'

'Let's see, shall we?' asked Bud, pushing himself up from the table.

He disappeared behind his section of the curtained-off bedroom, grabbed a pea coat and then went outside to throw an old saddle across a trim little Morgan colt. O'Brien and Temple followed him to the corral, leaving Don and Kathryn alone. Even from that distance, however, they could hear the couple's raised voices. The words themselves were muffled and indistinct, but clearly angry.

'Good luck,' said Temple as Bud led the horse out of the pen and O'Brien stepped up to leather and gathered his reins.

'We'll be back quick as we can,' said O'Brien. 'I doubt Quillan'll try anything straight away, but keep a lookout anyway.'

'Oh, you can bank on that,' Temple replied fervently. 'From now on, I don't think we can afford to leave a single thing to chance.'

* * *

'I might've known Chamberlain was in on it,' Bud growled as they rode fast toward town. 'Newton wouldn't've

124

dared show his face if he hadn't lured you out of the way first.'

'I'm not so sure,' O'Brien replied. 'He seemed like a straight shooter to me. And he read the riot act to Quillan.'

'You see him do that?'

'No. But I didn't see any reason to doubt him, either.'

'Well, you're entitled to your opinion,' allowed Bud. 'Let's just hope we don't need him, 'cause if we do, he'll show his true colors.'

'Seems to me everyone's made up their minds about Chamberlain.'

'But you haven't, is that it?'

'Not based on what I saw today.'

Twenty minutes later Sunrise came into sight. At Bud's suggestion, they left their horses in a crude cable corral about midway along Main, then he said, 'We'll check out The Temple of Bacchus first.'

'Sounds fancy.'

'It's not. It's a billiard hall that doubles as a saloon. Most wildcatters hang around there when they're lookin' for work.'

'All right. Lead on.'

The Temple of Bacchus was a large stained and much-repaired tent with a floor of loose boards laid over dirt and three scratched billiard tables set up between the entrance flap and a barrel-and-plank counter. The air smelled like burnt sugar and peyote tea, blackberry liquor and — unsettlingly — turpentine. A number of wildcatters were lined up at the bar, while others played cards or billiards for matches at the handful of tables on offer. All were really just hanging around for one thing — the chance that someone might come in and hire them.

Bud stopped in the entrance and scanned the customers through the fog of cigarette smoke that drifted around the lamps suspended from a central rafter. After a moment he made a small sound in his throat and gestured to a corner table at which three men were nursing drinks and playing brag without really thinking about it. One of the players was a broad-shouldered black man O'Brien recognized immediately — the man Bud had called Johnny Organ.

The wildcatter pushed through the crowds, headed directly for the table, and O'Brien followed behind him, automatically checking the place out for any signs of trouble. No one paid them much attention.

'Johnny-boy,' Bud said when he was near enough. 'Was hopin' I'd find you here.'

Johnny Organ had seen him coming. He stood up a little uncertainly, shook hands and nodded a greeting. He was about six feet tall, with broad shoulders that narrowed to a slim waist and long, powerful-looking arms and legs. His hair was a mass of thick tight curls, his skin the same color as mahogany, his features pleasant and well proportioned. The whites of his eyes were the palest yellow. The eyes themselves were a sharp polished brown, a little fogged now by alcohol.

'Nice to see you agin, Mr. Bishop,' he

said as they shook. 'I guess you heard about our misfortune?'

'I heard. Jenner was a good man, an' so was his brother. They deserved better.'

Johnny indicated the drinks on the table. 'Well, we're doin' what we can to send 'em both home in style.'

'So I see. Well, I don't like to intrude, so I'll come straight to it, then let you get back to your mournin'. I guess you're lookin' for work.'

'Yessir,' said Organ. 'Quillan, he laid us off the minute he took back ownership of the lease.'

'I heard that, too. Nate Newton came out to the Kathryn this mornin' and hired my men away from me to work it for him.'

'Word is,' said the negro, 'the Kathryn's gonna be a big one.'

'Big is right.'

'And you only got three days left to bring 'er in.'

'Uh-huh.'

'Which means it's another well

Quillan's got his eye on.'

Bud nodded. 'I won't dress it up, fellers. If I bring this well in, it'll be a gusher, all right. You all know me. You know I'm not greedy. Any man who helps me do it will find himself with the biggest bonus he's ever collected. But he'll earn it. That's why I'm paying fightin' wages to anyone who throws in with me.'

'Can you bring it in?'

'I can do it,' Bud replied. 'I'm so damn close now I can almost taste it. Three thousand, nine hundred feet. We *got* to hit it soon.'

The men at the table considered that. By their reckoning, Bud had already drilled about five hundred feet deeper than he should have had to. If there was oil there, surely it would have come to the surface by now ... But as Bud himself had said, they knew him, and knew his reputation. If he said oil was there, it was. And if he said it was going to be a gusher, it would be all of that, too.

'I'll work for you, Mr. Bishop,' said Johnny Organ. 'I like you, I trust you, I like the idea of a bonus at the end. But I liked Jeff an' Billy Jenner, too . . . and I reckon workin' for you's gonna give me the chance to get another crack at Quillan, he shows his face around your lease.'

'It is that, Johnny-boy.'

One of the other men said, 'Well, I only had the one experience at fightin', and that was night before last. Be honest with you, Mr. Bishop, I'm in no hurry to do it again . . . but I will, if it means gettin' another shot at Quillan.'

Bud nodded approvingly. 'Then you're hired, Haygood.' He studied the remaining man. 'What about you? It's Appleby, isn't it?'

'Yes, sir,' said Appleby, who at twenty-five was the youngest of the three. 'I'm in.'

Relieved, Bud hooked a thumb over his shoulder. 'Then say howdy to O'Brien, here. He's the man who's gonna fix Quillan's wheel for him. But if Quillan plays rough, like we 'spect him to, you'll all get your chance.'

They nodded a cautious greeting.

'Here,' said Bud, spilling some coins on the table. 'Drink a couple more to Jenner's memory, an' spend the rest of the afternoon soberin' up. We've pretty much lost today, but we'll work twice as hard tomorrow, to make up for it.'

Johnny Organ nodded. 'That we will,' he said. 'Anythin' else?'

O'Brien spoke for the first time. 'Don't forget your weapons,' he advised. 'And all the ammunition you can carry.'

★   ★   ★

It was well past lunchtime when they left The Temple of Bacchus, and Bud said he was hungry. They found a tent restaurant, ordered pork chops, corn fritters and baked beans, then took their piled plates to one of about half a dozen crowded trestle tables to eat.

Forking up food like it was going out of style, Bud said, 'Town like this, everyone stands to make money. But for some, there's no such thing as enough. Well, Quillan can do whatever he likes — he's not gettin' his hands on the Kathryn. I'll fight him every foot of the way, and then spit in his eye when he realizes I can buy and sell his sorry ass a dozen times over.'

O'Brien looked across the table at him. 'Keep it down,' he said.

Bud lowered his voice. 'I know it's not gonna be that easy,' he went on. 'But ain't no one takin' away my shot at glory now! I've spent my whole life bringin' in wells. Now I got the chance to bring in the biggest one of all, I'm not about to give it up without a fight. 'Sides . . . it's not just for me I'm doin' it.'

'No?'

'No. An' grateful though I am to Senator Norris and his backers, it's not for them, either. It's for Don.'

O'Brien chewed and swallowed. 'He's a good man,' he said.

'He's all of that. But you heard what Kathryn said, earlier on. He's not *me*.

132

And much as I love him, he never will be. But that's all right — I don't want him to be another me, I want him to be his own man . . . though it strikes me he'll never be enough man for her.'

Although he continued to listen, O'Brien's attention was taken by a newcomer who stopped and bent his head to two men who were seated down at the far end of the trestle table. The newcomer said something to them, hooked a thumb over one shoulder and then left again. The two men he'd addressed quickly finished their meal, then also took their leave.

'I know, I know,' Bud continued. 'I shouldn't get involved. Just let them work it out for themselves. And they will. But that's why I want to bring this well in, too. To set Don up in such a way that he won't have to spend his life in the oilfields, like I have . . . and so she'll have everything she wants, and no call to ever complain about him again.'

'Well, I'll buy you all the time I can to make it happen,' O'Brien replied, his mind still on the men who had left in such a hurry. 'You finished?'

'Just about.'

'All right. Let's make tracks.'

They collected their mounts from the public corral and had just started back along Main when Bud said, 'What do we have here, eh?'

O'Brien had already noticed the unusual number of men hurrying up toward The Christmas Tree, and disappearing down the alleyway between the saloon and the tent-store beside it. 'Nothing good, I'll bet,' he replied.

Bud leaned sideways out of his saddle and hailed a wildcatter who was also heading for the saloon. 'Say, feller! What's goin' on up at The Christmas Tree?'

The wildcatter grinned. 'Dog fight,' he replied. 'Out back.'

Bud nodded his thanks and growled to O'Brien, 'That's Quillan for you . . . he'll make money any way he can.'

By now there were almost up to the saloon, and could hear considerable noise filtering out onto Main from the open yard behind it. A dog was barking repeatedly, its excitement high. Impulsively O'Brien drew rein, and Bud walked his mount on a few paces before he realized he was alone. Turning at last, he said, 'What's up?'

O'Brien shook his head, unable to articulate what was really little more than a bad feeling. But it had paid him to heed such feelings in the past, more than once. 'Just wait for me a minute,' he said at last, and then swung down and handed Bud his reins.

He dodged wagons and riders to cross the street, and followed yet more wild-catters as they headed for the backyard. The yard turned out to be a cleared area bordered by stacked crates, piles of empty bottles and a stack of timber left over from the saloon's construction.

At least a hundred men had formed a rough circle and were laughing and conversing with each other. The expectancy in the air made O'Brien feel even more uneasy — or maybe it was that

135

constant snarling bark he could hear above everything else.

Eliciting scowls and curses from the men around him, he pushed toward the front of the circle. Dog fighting was not to his taste and never had been, just like the pitting of bears against bulls, as they did down in Mexico. More often than not it was slaughter, plain and simple.

Then he saw Nate Newton on the far side of the circle, holding Harry Chamberlain's dog, Eddie, on a short length of rope, and knew his disquiet had been justified. He quickly scanned the crowd for Chamberlain himself, but knew he wouldn't find him. No way would Chamberlain allow his dog to be used for this.

On the opposite side of the impromptu arena, a big man with pocked skin was bending over some kind of wolf dog, fingers tightened into its fur as he yelled at it to do its job, which was to rip and tear and kill. The wolf dog kept barking and snarling, and the big man kept twisting his fists into the flesh behind the dog's head and along its side, building its ferocity. Nearby, a minion of Quillan's was taking bets — not on who would win; there was no question about that; but on how long it would take the wolf dog to kill the water spaniel.

O'Brien looked back at the marshal's dog. Unnerved by all the noise, Eddie was struggling to get out of Newton's grasp. Watching Newton tighten his grip on the animal only made O'Brien's anger build. He scanned the crowd, spotted Quillan at the back, overseeing everything with that carefree grin of his, and then he was shoving through the crowd again, ignoring all complaints, until Quillan finally saw him coming.

'Ah, O'Brien,' he called. 'Ye jest can't leave us alone, can ye?'

O'Brien said, 'Call it off, Irish.'

'This?' Quillan asked, frowning. 'Not on your life, mack. Why, the lads want a little entertainment — you wouldn't begrudge them, now would ye?'

'You call it off,' said O'Brien. 'Or *I* will.'

'Now, that,' said Quillan, 'I'd like to see.'

'You don't have to do this,' O'Brien said.

'Oh, but I do,' Quillan argued easily. 'Y'see, when a man I put in a position of power tells me I'd better toe the line if I know what's good for me, well . . . that man needs teachin' a lesson.'

'So you kill his dog,' said O'Brien.

'I've told ye once,' said Quillan, 'a man has to be tough to survive in a town like this.'

Behind him, the yelling and laughter was reaching a pitch. Telling himself he was a damned fool, O'Brien turned, pushed through the crowd, and drew his Colt as he stepped into the circle. The single shot he fired into the air got everyone's attention, and suddenly all the banter, the laughter, the making of bets, died away.

'Forget it, fellers,' he called. 'There's not going to be any dog fight here today.'

A second passed, as the words sunk

in. Then the yelling started again, and this time it was angry and challenging.

'An' who the hell're you?' someone called.

Ignoring that, O'Brien strode across to Newton. Newton watched him come, shifty-eyed and nervous as ever. When he was close enough, O'Brien held out his free hand. 'I'll take the dog,' he said.

Newton, knowing he had the backing of the crowd on his side, risked a sneer. 'The hell you will,' he replied.

O'Brien's eyes were flat and dangerous. 'I'll take the dog,' he grated. 'Now.'

Newton tried to meet his gaze and couldn't. Instead, he turned his head and tried to seek guidance from Quillan, and while he was doing that, O'Brien tore the rope leash from his grip. 'Come on, Eddie.'

He turned, saw the big man with the pocked face ready to release the wolf dog and pointed the Colt at him. 'Try it,' he said. 'They can bury you both together.'

The man looked like he might take his chances. Around them the crowd went crazy for such a contest.

Then O'Brien sensed a sudden, expectant hush settling back behind him, and chanced a look over his shoulder just as Quillan swaggered into the cleared circle. The Irishman raised his hands for quiet, and after a moment it fell silent again, but for the never-ending *thump . . . thump . . . thump . . .* coming from the oilfield.

'Ye've spoilt our fun, an' no mistake,' he said. 'But before ye get too despondent, lads, it could be that O'Brien here'll provide more entertainment than the dogs.'

O'Brien moved back so that he could keep Quillan, Newton and the man with the pocked face in view. 'Forget it,' he said. 'I'm taking this dog out of here and I'll shoot the first man who tries to stop me.'

'Will ye now?' asked Quillan. 'And how far d'ye think ye'll get, one against a hundred, if not more, and all of 'em with their bloodlust up?' He turned toward the big man with the pocked face. 'What say we switch dogs for men, eh, Nolan?'

The pock-faced man grinned coldly, showing jagged stumps for teeth. 'Just let me at him,' he said. He turned and thrust the wolf dog's leash at one of his companions, then stepped into the circle. He was about thirty, and stood at least six feet six inches. Beneath an old knitted cap he was bald, his features clustered together in the center of his face. He didn't have a neck — his shoulders seemed to slope down from just beneath his ears — and his chest was broad and powerful. Big arms, big fists, thick, tree-trunk legs that might slow him down in a fight but would support him all the way through the contest.

O'Brien looked up at him and again cursed himself for a fool. He'd given Quillan exactly the chance he'd been looking for — the chance to have him beaten so badly there wouldn't be any way he could ride shotgun on the Bishop well. But what else was he supposed to do, sacrifice the marshal's dog?

'Come on, ye spalpeen!' called Nolan, bringing his fists up.

O'Brien thought of his healing ribs and other assorted hurts, and knew he would be lucky to last a minute against such a powerful opponent. But what the hell — you never knew your luck.

Mouth thinning down, he looked around for someone to pass Eddie's leash to.

And that was when Bud Bishop shouldered through the crowd and said, 'Gimme some room, O'Brien. I'll take care o' this.'

7

Not waiting for an answer, Bud swept off his derby hat and flung it aside. If he knew what he was letting himself in for, he gave no indication of it. It didn't seem to matter to him that he was about to pit himself against a fitter, stronger man half his age — it was as if he couldn't get into combat quick enough.

O'Brien said, 'Bud . . . '

'Marquess of Queensbury?' Bud interrupted, addressing Quillan.

Quillan's grin broadened. O'Brien or Bud, it made no difference to him. Break one or break both, and the Bishop well would be his for the taking. 'Flame an' thunder,' he replied, and seemed to savor every word.

Bud shrugged. 'Come on, then, Nolan,' he said, and crooked a finger at his opponent. 'Let's be havin' you.'

Nolan came forward, heavy-footed, left fist up to guard his face, right fist held lower, to protect his stomach. Bud danced away from him, surprisingly nimble for his weight, his own fists moving in tight circles.

Nolan leapt forward and caught him with a straight jab. In the expectant silence, it made a meaty smack of sound and O'Brien winced, figuring to step in the minute it looked as if Nolan had the beating of the older man. Sensing blood, the crowd went wild, cheering, jeering, eagerly placing bets on the outcome.

But Bud only shook his head a little, grinned, brought his hands up again and said, 'That the best you got, Nolan?'

Nolan came at him again, tried to kick him on the shin. Bud danced back, out of reach, then came in fast, and all at once he was like a powerhouse, jabbing, first left, then right, then left again, hitting Nolan in the ribs, working his way up toward the head.

144

Startled, Nolan started backing up, tucking his elbows into his sides, head bobbing and weaving as he sought a chance to fight back.

Not finding one, he crowded Bud and tried to knee him in the crotch. Bud moved back a little and the knee caught him a glancing blow in the stomach instead. He danced back, face beet-red and slick with sweat, shoulders rising and falling fast as he sought to catch his breath. Nolan saw as much and came in quickly, determined not to give him the chance.

Then it was Bud's turn to go on the defensive, and though he did well he didn't quite manage to block all the jabs and uppercuts that came his way. When Nolan caught him it was with hard, forceful blows that rocked him from side to side, and when the big man danced back, there were bruises and swellings already rising around Bishop's brow and jaw.

Bud dragged down a breath, spat blood off to one side. A line of it dribbled sluggishly down the side of his face from a split near his eyebrow.

Then they went at it again, throwing themselves at each other and trading punch for punch, and around them the crowd was galvanized. Men cheered and yelled half-assed advice. Nolan's wolf dog barked non-stop. It was almost enough to drown out the thumping of the derricks, but O'Brien, watching, feeling the dog in his care shivering all the way up the leash to his hand, still felt each nauseating blow beneath his feet.

Bud hooked a punch to Nolan's belly. Nolan took it and laughed about it. He threw a straight right back at Bud, and Bud saw it coming, slapped it aside and threw a right cross at Nolan's lantern jaw. Nolan staggered under the impact, and Bud went after him, caught him with a left uppercut, then used the right again and slammed it hard against Nolan's nose.

O'Brien knew a moment of elation then. Few men have the will to keep fighting when they're nursing a broken nose. Nolan tried. Blood streaming from his nostrils, he roared and threw himself back at Bud, swinging wildly. Bud ducked and came up inside his guard, grabbed Nolan's shirtfront and pulled him down so that he could butt him with his forehead.

Nolan went mad with pain, backed off, came in again, his nose swelling fast now, forcing him to breathe through his mouth. He was jabbing, hooking, throwing uppercuts and roundhouse swings in a desperate attempt to finish Bud, but Bud seemed to have got his second wind, was showboating a little as he danced back and dodged to left or right, making Nolan look like a fool.

And with a sudden flash of insight O'Brien realized that this had been Bud's strategy all along — to get his opponent good and mad, turn him into a laughingstock and make him careless. It was working.

Nolan heeled around with his fists folded, but Bud was right there waiting for him. He punched low, caught Nolan between the legs, and Nolan went up and howled, stumbled back and almost fell. He turned to the man holding his dog. The wolf dog was straining to enter the fray and get the man who was beating his master. He opened his mouth and gestured that the dog should be released, but O'Brien cocked his Colt, aimed it at the man and shook his head.

Then Bud came in and hit Nolan again, on the right ear. Nolan sagged, dropped to his knees, and Bud hit him again, again, one more time, and finally Nolan's eyes rolled up in his head and he fell like a sack of grain onto his side.

If anything, the mixture of cheering and booing increased. Bud stood over his opponent, belly swelling and contracting as he sucked down air. His knuckles were split and bleeding. His brow had swollen so that it overhung his eyes. He backhanded blood from his nose, and it smeared across one cheek like strawberry preserve. He turned, raised his hands to acknowledge the adulation of the crowd, and amazingly he found it in him to laugh, actually *laugh*, as if he'd just had the time of his life.

Keeping his gun out, O'Brien jerked on Eddie's leash and crossed the yard. 'Get your hat, Bud,' he hissed. 'And let's get the hell out of here while we can.'

Bud glanced at him, his eyes alight. 'I could stand a drink,' he said. 'And these fellers'll be linin' up to buy 'em for us.'

'You can drink when we're back at the well.'

Bud shrugged, scooped up his derby and set it at just the right jack-deuce angle on his head. But Quillan, who'd overheard their exchange, quickly plucked a glass from one of the onlookers. Determined not to lose any more face than he already had, he thrust the glass out to Bud, a little beer spilling over the rim as he did so.

Suddenly it went quiet.

A moment passed, and then Bud

accepted the glass.

He took off his hat and slowly poured the beer over his head.

At once the crowd started roaring again, and Quillan's face tightened with anger.

But the action had confirmed Bud as the hero of the hour, and there were no shortage of hearty backslaps as they he followed O'Brien and Eddie back out onto Main.

★ ★ ★

Harry Chamberlain was dozing behind his desk when they reached the law office and let themselves inside. The marshal grunted and sat up quickly, trying to look fresh and alert. He saw O'Brien first, then Bud . . . and then Eddie.

Curiously, he said to the dog, 'I was wonderin' where you'd gotten to.'

O'Brien untied the crude leash and Eddie scurried across to his master, claws crackling against the board floor.

'He was about to be guest of honor at

a dog fight,' O'Brien told him.

Chamberlain stared at him a moment, then looked at Bud's still-flushed face, with its bumps and cuts. 'You got him out of it,' he said.

'Uh-huh.'

'Quillan?' said the marshal.

'Seems he didn't cotton much to the way you talked to him this morning.'

Chamberlain's face went tight, and without warning the sadness in his eyes was replaced by something dark and dangerous that transformed him completely. 'That's too bad,' he said softly.

He stood up, shifted the weight of his gunbelt a little and reached for his Stetson.

'Not so fast, Marshal,' said O'Brien. 'Go looking for a fight with Quillan now and he'll cut you down and find someone else to pack your star.'

'He's likely to do that, anyway. He's already let me have it chapter and verse — how I shouldn't forget my place, or overstep the mark. It didn't faze me then, either.'

'Then you've made your choice?' asked O'Brien. 'About who you'll be siding when the war breaks out?'

Chamberlain scrubbed affectionately at the dog's long ears. 'I'll be there when the shootin' starts, don't fret,' he said quietly.

Bud made a short, disparaging sound in his throat. Chamberlain eyed him sharply. 'You got somethin' you want to spit out?' he asked.

Bud said, 'You better not let us down, that's all.'

Chamberlain opened his mouth to reply, then changed his mind. Instead he said, very softly, 'Looks like you took some bruises on Eddie's account, Bishop. For that, an' for fetchin' him home again, I'm obliged. But don't you ever use that tone with me again, you got it?'

Bishop squared his shoulders. 'Grown a backbone, have you?'

'What I've grown,' sighed Chamberlain, 'is sick of people like you, who listen to half-assed rumors and take 'em as gospel.' His eyes shifted to O'Brien and some of the iron went out of them. 'Obliged to you, too, O'Brien.'

'Keep an eye on him from now on,' O'Brien said with a gesture toward the dog. 'And watch *your* back, too — because it just became a target.'

⋆ ⋆ ⋆

It was coming on dusk when the well came into sight, silhouetted against a sullen gray sky. The ride back had been largely silent, but now Bud groaned and shifted in the saddle as he tried to ease his spine. 'Stiffenin' up,' he croaked.

'It'll pass.'

'That it will. Any case, it was worth it. We showed that damn Quillan, didn't we?'

'You did, sure. But it won't end there.'

'Be surprised if he did. Still, we'll be ready for him. Got the new crew comin' out tomorrow.'

'Just don't forget we've still got to get

through tonight.'

The sounds of their approach brought Temple, Don and Kathryn out of the dugout, Don carrying his shotgun across his chest. They watched as O'Brien and Bud turned their horses into the corral, and then Bud stepped into the trough and sat down, fully clothed, in the cold water.

'What the hell . . . ?' began Don.

'Save it for later,' called Bud. 'Right now, all I want to do is soak my hurts.' Temple looked at O'Brien. 'What happened?'

O'Brien told it in a few sentences. At the end Temple shook his head and said, 'I thought you were supposed to keep him out of trouble!'

'Ah, quit chewin' leather!' called Bud. 'Nobody forced me to take a hand, I just did!'

'But you put this entire enterprise at risk — '

'Oh, forget it, Temple, it's history, man!' Bud climbed out of the trough and stamped across the shadow cast by the derrick, leaving a trail of water behind him. Already he was stripping off his shirt. 'Kath, fetch some axle grease an' help me fix these cuts. Better break out the vinegar for my achin' muscles while you're at it, an' arnica for these here bruises.'

Don broke his long silence. 'I'll do it.'

'Kath can do it,' Bud insisted, with no understanding of the embarrassment to which he might be subjecting the girl. 'She's got smaller hands and a lighter touch — an' you need to keep watch.'

'But — '

'It's all right, Don,' she said, her tone resigned. 'I'll do it.'

'O'Brien — ' began Temple.

'It worked out for the best,' O'Brien told him. 'We got Jenner's old crew — they'll be starting work first thing in the morning. Plus, we made a friend out of Chamberlain — '

'Oh, we're all right then,' Temple said sarcastically. 'We've got Chamberlain on our side!'

155

O'Brien said softly, 'Don't be so quick to write him off, Jim. You staying out here tonight?'

'I need to talk to Bud,' the attorney replied. 'It'll probably be best if I stay over now, and go back to town tomorrow.'

'Then sleep light,' said O'Brien. 'You too, Don.'

Don came closer. 'You think we'll have trouble?'

'I know we will,' O'Brien replied. 'We might be running out of time to bring this well in, but Quillan's running out of time, too — to make sure we don't make it.' He nodded. 'Oh, yeah. As sure as guns are iron . . . we'll have trouble.'

★   ★   ★

Supper was a subdued affair. Only Bud seemed oblivious to the mood around the table. Having been patched up by Kathryn, he'd changed into clean clothes and concentrated on his food, eating with relish. After cleaning his own plate, O'Brien took his leave. He stood for a while in the darkness outside, listening to the wind. In the distance, toward Sunrise, he heard the drills *thump . . . thump . . . thumping* in their endless quest to strike oil. He studied their lonely surroundings, tested the air with his nose, then crossed the lease toward the tent. There he took a cot, stretched out with his Winchester close at hand, and caught some rest ahead of what he expected to be a long, sleepless night.

About an hour later Temple entered the tent and, figuring that O'Brien was asleep, helped himself to another cot and was soon snoring softly. O'Brien got up, and with Winchester in hand, took a slow walk around the perimeter of the lease. It was, by his reckoning, about ten o'clock, and silence had finally claimed the land.

He turned and went to the stacked lumber behind which he'd taken cover the day before, having already decided that it was the best place from which to keep watch. Although the late-fall days in these parts were still as hot as desert rocks, the nighttime temperatures dropped dramatically. Tonight was no exception, and he was glad he'd decided to wear his wolfskin jacket.

He looked over at the dugout. It was in darkness. A scuffling sound off to his left made him turn and narrow his eyes. A few seconds later a raccoon waddled into the moonlight and he smiled. A few minutes after that the air was rent by the drawn-out *woo-oo-hoo* of a coyote.

Without warning he caught a scent of lavender and sandalwood and turned to see Kathryn crossing the lease with a tray in her hands, a coffeepot and mug glinting in the moonlight. She was headed for the tent until O'Brien stood up and blew a low whistle. Then she turned, saw him, and he in turn saw her shoulders drop a little in relief. She changed direction and hurried toward him.

'I thought you could probably use some coffee,' she said softly, when she was near enough.

'You thought right.'

He set the Winchester aside and took the tray from her, set it down and poured a cup.

'Thank you, ma'am,' he said.

'Don't thank me,' she said. 'I was glad for the excuse to get out of there. Don snoring his head off next to me, Bud groanin' every time he turns one way or the other.'

'Well, I appreciate the thought, anyway.'

He expected her to go back to the dugout. She didn't. Instead she looked out over the moon-washed meadow and said, 'Do you really think we'll have trouble tonight?'

'I'll be surprised if we don't. Which is why you'd better go back inside and stay under cover.'

'In a while,' she said, and looked up at the stars. 'Given the choice, I'd sooner take my chances out here.'

'Wouldn't your husband have something to say about that, Mrs. Bishop?'

Through the darkness her teeth showed in a sudden, short-lived smile. 'You can call me Kathryn, if you like,' she said. 'As for Don . . . don't tell me you're afraid of what *he* thinks?'

'I reckon he'd prefer you to be safe inside.'

'I'm safe enough with you, aren't I, Mr. O'Brien?'

Because he knew where she wanted this to go, he faced her head on and said firmly, 'Yes, ma'am. Safe as a blockhouse.'

She got the message, and hated it. In the darkness she deflated a notch, then looked out across the lease again. 'Well, you can't blame me lookin' for a little excitement,' she said. 'Lord knows, there's not much to be had around here.'

'No, ma'am, I guess there isn't. But it won't always be that way. When Bud brings this well in, you'll be rich. You could go east, live a better life.'

'No I couldn't. Because it's not about the money for those two, and it never was — it's about *oil*, forcin' it up out of the ground. It was always that way for Bud, and the one thing you can say about Don is that he's his father's boy. He wants to be just like Bud, carry on the family business. Well . . . Bud's wife put up with it till she died, but not *this* child. I want somethin' more than livin' rough and ready, and patchin' up an ugly old man who thinks I'm invisible till he's got a use for me — ' She bit off, looked at him again. 'I thought maybe you could — '

O'Brien made a hissing sound that shut her right up, and turned so suddenly that instinctively she drew back from him.

Out in the darkness, the coyote's cry had changed from *woo-oo-hoo* to a series of barks that ended in a howl, and O'Brien had spent enough time outdoors to know what that meant.

'Someone's coming,' he whispered.

8

The coyote's cry of warning started off the entire pack. Listening to the way the howls changed but not understanding why, Kathryn said, 'How do you know — '

'Shhh!'

Not taking his eyes off their surroundings, he reached out, found her shoulder, and pushed her none too gently down behind the timber. Aside from the distant howling of the coyotes, the night was quiet again.

Then one of the horses in the corral shook its head and blew air through its nostrils. For a man who knew how to read them, it was another warning sign.

He turned his head slowly and focused on a spot just to one side of the corral, knowing he would see more from the edge of his vision than he would if he looked directly at his objective. Nothing moved except the horses, as they stamped and shifted restlessly.

Then a shadow detached itself from beside the wagon next to the corral.

The shadow of a man.

He ghosted across the lease, hugging something close to his chest as he moved in a cautious crouch-walk. Kathryn caught her breath. The man was heading for the engine house.

O'Brien jacked a shell into the Winchester. The sound was magnified by the silence. As the man in the center of the lease stopped dead, O'Brien yelled, 'That's far enough!'

Twisting, the man brought up and fired a handgun at the sound of O'Brien's voice. Even as the bullet smacked into the far side of the stacked timber, O'Brien brought the Winchester stock to his cheek, snap-aimed and dropped hammer.

As O'Brien's bullet hit the dynamite the man had been carrying, the deadly mixture of nitroglycerin, absorbent earth and sodium carbonate went off with a deep bellow of sound. The man himself vanished in a fireball without even time to scream, and a wave of furnace-heat blasted out in all directions.

Kathryn screamed.

For a split second night turned into day and the ground tipped beneath them. O'Brien ducked, covered Kathryn, dropped the Winchester and folded his arms over his head as the sound of the detonation slammed at them.

Seconds later he was up again, in time to see a great burst of flame, white-orange at its heart, black and greasy on its underside, rise up into the night sky.

Kathryn began to rise. Snatching the Winchester back up, he told her to stay where she was. The dynamite was no surprise, leastways not to him. It had, after all, been Quillan's specialty. Temple had told him as much the day before. But that hadn't been Quillan out there just now, though. He wouldn't handle dirty work himself while he had others to do it for —

Even as he thought it, the rest of Quillan's men, the five who'd been waiting out in the darkness for the dynamite man to place his sticks and blow the engine house, came galloping in out of the night, some firing handguns, the rest hurling flaming torches at every available target.

At once the lease came roaring to life. As the corralled horses began to circle ever more nervously, Bud and Don pounded out of the dugout with weapons in hand. They took one look at the horsemen cantering through camp, then threw themselves behind cover and set about returning fire. A torch landed on the roof of the tent and the flames immediately took hold. Temple stumbled out into the night, someone took a shot at him and he quickly threw himself down, out of sight.

Having hurled his torch into a pile of tarpaulins, one of the Quillan men turned his mount, dragged a Colt from its holster and kneed his horse back to a run, firing wildly, first left, then right. O'Brien came up from behind the timber, tracked him, led him a little and squeezed the trigger. The man rode straight into the bullet and it clubbed him sideways out of his saddle, blood geysering from a wound where his right ear had been.

Another rider went by and Don leveled his Moore & Company shotgun. Flame spat from one barrel and the recoil threw him back a step, but the load — one twelfth of a pound of lead shot — backhanded the rider off the far side of his mount.

The rider hit the ground hard and his hat came off. O'Brien saw by the light of the fires a flash of a red hair, and knew that this was Newton's companion, the one who'd vanished into the saloon's backyard with the intention of shooting him from ambush.

He jacked in another round, fired at a man who came galloping to the redhead's aid, but Kathryn chose that moment to grab at his legs and the shot missed. The redhead staggered to his feet, his shredded arm hanging limp at his side, and his companion heaved him astride his horse before they both lit out into the surrounding darkness.

Their surviving comrades were of the same mind, but Bishop wasn't about to let them get off that lightly. His fighting blood up again, he broke cover, planted himself in the center of the lease and emptied his carbine into the escaping riders. He missed the one he'd been aiming at but hit his horse instead. With a scream that sounded all too human, the animal went down and over in a forward roll, crushing its rider beneath it.

Then they were gone, the sound of their fading hooves following them back into the night.

O'Brien yelled, 'Get some water on those fires! I'll keep watch, make sure they don't come back!'

Though shaken by the recent violence, Temple hurried to the trough to do as O'Brien had said. After a moment Bud went to join him. But Don remained where he was, glaring across the lease at O'Brien.

It took him a moment to understand why. Then —

Kathryn. She was standing beside him now, shocked to the core.

But there was no time to explain things right then. Kathryn saw that, even if Don didn't. She too ran toward the trough, and eventually he joined the others there . . . but not before he'd given O'Brien another look that promised murder.

* * *

It was a long night. The drizzle that started to fall a little after midnight made it seem even longer.

O'Brien patrolled the perimeter of the lease while Kathryn and Temple put out the fires before they could do much damage, and Bud and Don rigged out some horses with chains and dragged the dead animal out of the yard and into the cedars two hundred yards away. The carcass would doubtless feed the coyotes and such few wolves as there were in those parts.

They also wrapped the dead men and what remained of the dynamite man in blankets and left those in the same area. If time allowed, they'd bury them later.

The wall tent had been burned beyond repair, but fortunately the cots and O'Brien's gear had remained untouched. The engine house had suffered some damage from the dynamite blast, but Bishop said he would have to wait for daylight to make sure nothing serious had happened to the donkey engine itself.

'Will they be back in the meantime, do you think?' asked Temple, coming out to find him when he and Kathryn had done as much as they could.

'I doubt it. But we'll be in better shape when Jenner's old crew shows up. They know we're in for a fight of it — Bud made sure of that — and they're game for it.'

'And if they don't show up?'

O'Brien looked at him. The possibility hadn't even occurred to him. 'They didn't strike me as men who'd give their word lightly — or men who'd allow Quillan to throw another scare into them, comes to that.' He turned his steps back toward the derrick. 'Come on. Let's take one of the undamaged tarpaulins and rig up a new shelter for Jenner's crew.'

'Me and Mr. Temple here can see to that,' said Bud, who had caught the last of their conversation as he climbed down from the engine. 'You go inside and get some rest, O'Brien. You can use my cot.' When he hesitated, Bud added, 'You'll be no good to man or beast if you're dead on your feet.'

'I'll give you no argument there,' O'Brien replied. As the sky began to lighten, and the prospect of further trouble diminished, he headed for the dugout.

★　★　★

Inside, he threw his hat onto the table and shoved the right-side blanket-curtain back on its crude rope slide. Bud's sleeping quarters was little more than a narrow cot screened off from Don and Kathryn's by another thick wool blanket hung from the low dirt ceiling. Privacy for the young couple must be practically non-existent, he thought. He lay down and closed his eyes, trying to work out what Quillan would most likely do next. As the sun continued to rise, he finally allowed himself to relax a little and dozed off.

The opening and closing of the half-glass door woke him. He looked up as Don came inside, glanced at him, then sat down and rolled himself a smoke.

'Never shot a man before,' the younger man said after a moment. 'Never expected to.'

'It's a lousy feeling,' O'Brien allowed. 'And it doesn't get any easier. Leastways, it never did for me. But it was kill or get killed, Don. Times like that, you don't have much say in it.'

Don blew smoke at the ceiling. 'I hated it,' he said. 'But I'd do it again, if I had cause.' At last he looked at O'Brien again. 'You get my drift?' he asked.

O'Brien, in no mood to play games, sat up slowly. 'Can't say as I do.'

'All right,' said Don, twisting in the chair to face him. 'I don't know what my wife was doing out there with you last night, but it had better not be what I think it was.'

'Your wife brought me some coffee,' O'Brien replied. 'You don't believe me, go take a look behind that stacked timber. You find the pot and a cup on a tray. She was there when Quillan's men made their move. I told her to stay there and keep her head down until it was over. Satisfied?'

Don looked away from him, because it was easier to do that than to meet his steady gaze. 'I'm just sayin',' he muttered, but without much conviction now.

O'Brien looked at him and suddenly understood that it wasn't so much that Don didn't trust him; it was that he didn't trust her. But that was none of his business and he knew better than to involve himself in it. Even so, he said, as casually as he could manage, 'Maybe you and Kathryn should get away from here for a spell, after your dad brings the well in.'

Don laughed harshly. 'You're kidding, right? Bringing the well in is only the start of it. Once we've got the well producing, that's when the real work begins.'

He'd barely finished speaking when O'Brien came up off the cot. Don frowned at him. 'What's wrong?'

'Riders coming in,' he said.

They went outside just as Johnny Organ and the young man named Appleby rode in, well armed and with their gear tied behind their cantles. Bishop left Temple and Kathryn putting the finish touches to the crude tarpaulin-tent they'd rigged up and trotted over.

'Johnny, me boy!' he called. 'Come ahead and put your horses in the corral! Have you boys had anything to eat yet? Kathryn there — that's Don's wife — she makes the best pancakes you ever tasted!'

Johnny Organ looked around. "Pears to me you've had some trouble,' he said.

'Ah, we took care of it. Quillan sent some men out, but we put a flea in their ear.'

'So I see.'

'Well, what you waitin' for?' Bud demanded. 'Cool your saddles and we'll break bread. Then we'll get this well back up an' runnin'!' He turned at the waist. 'Kath! Kath, we got two hungry mouths here! Get yourself busy, girl!' He realized then that one man was missing. 'Where's Haygood?' he asked.

'He met with another one o' Quillan's accidents,' Johnny said grimly.

'No!'

The negro nodded. 'I don't know how word got around that we was comin' to work for you, but it did. They caught Haygood all by hisself an' that sonofabitch Newton broke his leg with an iron pipe. I guess they figgered that'd be a warnin' to Appleby an' me, but all it did was make us madder.'

'The bastard,' Bud grated. 'Haygood bein' looked after?'

'He'll live,' said Johnny. 'But he won't ever work the oilfields again.'

After the wildcatters had seen to their horses and stowed their gear, Bud gave them a quick tour of the lease and then started checking the donkey engine for damage. They found a ruptured steam valve but Bud didn't think it was anything they couldn't fix. Then they joined O'Brien for breakfast in the dugout.

Afterwards, Johnny and Appleby set about fixing the donkey engine. Watching them work, O'Brien asked Temple if he was going back to town. The attorney grimaced. 'That might not be such a good idea,' he replied. 'The next couple of days are going to be rough, aren't they? On everyone?'

'Uh-huh.'

'Then I'll stay here and pitch in.'

'What about your fiance back home in Maryland?'

'She'll understand,' said Temple, 'if I come through it in one piece.'

It was heading toward ten o'clock when another rider appeared in the distance — Harry Chamberlain, with the water spaniel, Eddie, sprawled lazily across his lap like a rescued calf. O'Brien and Temple walked out to meet him.

'Light a spell,' called O'Brien as Chamberlain drew rein.

The spaniel leapt down, sniffed at O'Brien's cords and then started wagging his tail. Chamberlain swung down slowly, a man no longer used to riding far. 'Coffee'd come welcome about now,' he allowed.

'Sure. Come on up to the dugout.'

Bud was so busy working on the donkey engine that he didn't even notice Chamberlain's arrival. Don saw him, though, and joined them as they went inside. With barely a word of greeting, Kathryn automatically poured coffee for everyone.

'Sweetenin'?' she asked, reaching for a pack of sugar on the shelf above the stove.

Chamberlain shook his head. 'Never touch it.'

She shrugged listlessly and then left them alone.

'I hear tell that Red Taylor got shot last night,' the marshal said, nudging his hat back. 'Took an arm full of buckshot.'

O'Brien said guilelessly, 'Who's Red Taylor?'

'One of Quillan's gunnies. Used to be, anyways. I doubt Quillan's got any further use for a gunman who's lost his gun-arm.'

Don made a small choking sound in his throat.

'What's that got to do with us?' asked O'Brien.

Chamberlain smiled. 'He hit you last

night, didn't he? Quillan, I mean. An' before you try to deny it, I can see the damage outside with my own eyes — not to mention the bodies you dragged off into them trees.'

Again O'Brien felt a strong liking for the old lawman.

'Looks to me like you won the first round,' Chamberlain observed.

'Wasn't so good for a feller named Haygood. Quillan had Newton break one of his legs before he could come out here and work with us.'

'I heard about that, too,' Chamberlain said gravely. He savored the coffee for a moment, then added, 'I reckon Quillan an' me'll be havin' words when I get back to town.'

'Don't go against him, Marshal,' warned O'Brien. 'Do that and you're out of a job.'

'And if I let him get away with it?'

'You keep the job, you become our man on the inside. Could be we'll have need of a good lawman sooner or later.'

Chamberlain chuckled dryly. 'All I

need is for you to swear charges against Quillan. I'll do the rest.'

'You'll get yourself killed, is what you'll do,' argued Temple. 'In any case, how can we prove Quillan was behind it? Knowing it's one thing — proving it's something else again.'

'Well, that sonofabitch owes me,' Chamberlain said grimly, reaching down to stroke the spaniel's head. 'Him an' that Newton both.'

'He owes us all,' Don reminded him.

'Then make sure he pays,' Chamberlain replied. 'And when the time comes due, don't you dare leave me out of it.' He turned to O'Brien. 'Any ideas how you're gonna get 'er done, O'Brien?'

'The main thing is to hold the lease long enough for Bud to bring the well in. If he can do that, I'd like to think Quillan would back off.'

'He won't.'

'No. So sooner or later, it's going to come to me and him, and shooting.'

'Well, like I said — don't you dare leave me out of it.'

As they watched the marshal ride slowly back toward Sunrise, Temple said, 'Quillan's men will be back tonight, won't they?'

'Most likely,' O'Brien replied. 'And this time they'll hit us just as hard as they can.'

While the others digested that, he looked around and made a swift calculation.

'There's six of us, not counting Kathryn,' he said. 'All right — we'll divide tonight up into three, three-hour stretches, and we'll keep two men on watch at all times. Don — spread the word.'

Don stared at him for a moment, still thinking about Kathryn, still wondering what Kathryn and O'Brien had been doing out there in the darkness last night.

'Don?'

At last he nodded and walked off toward the donkey engine.

'What's wrong with him?' asked Temple.

'Nothing,' O'Brien answered shortly. 'See you later.'

'Where are you going?'

'Clean my guns,' O'Brien replied. 'Then bury those bodies out there.'

★   ★   ★

He'd just finished digging a shallow communal grave for the three dead men when he heard the donkey engine splutter to life, followed by a cheer from Bud and the wildcatters who'd helped him fix it. So, he thought, they were back in business. Now it was all up to Bud to strike oil before the deadline.

It was late afternoon by the time he finished his grisly chore, and he was just tamping down the last of the damp earth when he heard a distant cry from the direction of the lease. Turning, he saw that a rider was coming in from the direction of town, a white kerchief held high above his head. When he recognized the man as Nate Newton, he thrust the shovel into the dirt, drew his Lightning and jogged out to cut him off.

'That's far enough!' he called.

Spotting him, Newton angled toward him, then tightened rein when no more than eight feet separated them. His bay and white paint horse came to a halt.

'What do you want?' O'Brien asked.

Newton grinned a tight, nervy grin that vanished almost as soon as it appeared. If he felt any remorse at all over breaking a man's leg with an iron pipe, he kept it very well hidden. 'Quillan's got an offer for you,' he said, his voice still a little distorted by his swollen jaw. 'Here.'

He threw an unsealed envelope down at O'Brien's feet.

O'Brien glanced at it. 'What's that?'

'Read it an' find out,' said Newton. 'You want to avoid any more grief, you got until first light tomorrow mornin' to get the hell off this lease.'

Having delivered his threat, he yanked his horse in a tight circle and gave it spurs. The paint galloped back toward Sunrise.

O'Brien bent and scooped up the

envelope. Inside was a single sheet of paper, upon which had been written:

A KATHRYN FOR A KATHRYN

Something in him went cold. 'What the hell was that all about?' He turned as Don — whose yell had first warned him of Newton's arrival — hustled up to him. 'Where's Kathryn?' he barked.

Don shrugged. 'Around here some-place — '

'Are you sure?'

'Sure I'm sure! Anyway, what did that sonofabitch want here? You should've shot him, after what he did to — '

O'Brien thrust the note at him to shut him up. 'Kathryn,' he said, and anger began to burn in him as he added, 'I think she's been kidnapped.'

9

No one had seen her since she'd served coffee and then walked out shortly after Marshal Chamberlain's arrival. Worse still, no one had even missed her until just before Don had gone into the dugout half an hour earlier to ask her about coffee and sandwiches for the men.

'I just figured she went off someplace to be by herself,' he said, his voice catching a little. 'It wouldn't be the first time. She was always — '

'Dammit!' raged Bud, punching one of the derrick beams. 'We should'a known that bastard'd try something like this!'

'None of you saw her wander off?' asked O'Brien.

'No.'

'And none of you saw anyone around here who shouldn't have been here?'

'Only Chamberlain, this morning,' said Don.

'An' how far can you trust him?' added Johnny Organ.

O'Brien squared his shoulders. 'You can trust him,' he said softly.

'Aw, fer crissakes, O'Brien,' snapped Bud, 'get it through your skull! He's Quillan's man! An' now we got no choice but to do like Quillan says, if we want to get Kath back safe an' sound!'

'Unless I get her back first,' said Don. Unable to contain himself any longer, he took a pace toward the corral. O'Brien's hand lashed out, wrapping around his wrist like an iron shackle.

'You're not going anywhere,' he said. 'None of you are.'

'The hell with you! That's my wife they've kidnapped!'

'And she'll be safe as long as Quillan needs her.'

'Safe? With *that* sonofa — ?'

'Use your head, Don! She's his bargaining chip. And as long as she's of use to him, he'll make sure no harm comes to her.'

'So what do we do in the meantime?'

asked Bud. 'I hate to give in, but I don't see's how we've got much choice, short of going into town an' takin' her back by force.'

'I'll get her back,' O'Brien said quietly.

'Hell with that!' Don exploded. 'She's my wife — '

'And you go after her the state you're in right now, you'll risk her life for sure,' O'Brien pointed out. 'Same with the rest of you.'

Johnny Organ muttered something under his breath, and O'Brien threw him a look. 'I know you're spoiling to get even for what happened to Jenner,' he said. 'Well, you'll have your way soon enough. But not yet. Not while Kathryn's life's at stake.'

Temple nodded. 'O'Brien's right,' he said. 'A thing like this . . . well, that's why we hired him.'

Don looked down at his boots for a moment, willing himself to simmer down. At last he looked up again, and staring at O'Brien, said, 'All right

— what are you going to do?'

O'Brien told him some of it . . . but he didn't dare tell it all.

★   ★   ★

It was sometime around midnight when the lady pianist finally quit for the night, and the last of The Christmas Tree's boozy customers staggered out onto Main and headed for home.

O'Brien watched them from the shadows of the alley beside the Sunflower Hotel, then looked up and read the time by the position of the gibbous moon. The night was cold, and every so often he had to flex his fingers to keep them working.

For the last half-hour or so, the sounds of merriment had been steadily tapering off inside the saloon, and drunken or just plain merry wildcatters had been leaving singly and in stumbling groups ever since.

It was, he thought, almost time to move.

Not that he really had much of a plan. Earlier on, he'd saddled the blood-bay and checked the area around the lease for anyone who might be keeping the place under observation. Not finding anyone, he'd returned and told Bud and the others to keep drilling. At that, Don's temper had snapped again, and this time they'd nearly come to blows. Bud and Johnny Organ had had to restrain Don while O'Brien explained his reasoning.

'Right now, you can't afford *not* to drill!' he'd said. 'If you bring this well in right now, today, Quillan's finished. He won't have any choice but to let Kathryn go.'

'You don't know that!'

'I know he'll have nothing to gain by continuing to hold her,' he replied. 'And even less reason to harm her.'

'So we keep drillin',' said Bud, seeing the sense to it, 'and you . . . ?'

'I go into The Christmas Tree and take her back,' he said.

'Just like that?' scoffed Don.

O'Brien bit back a profanity. This was no time for anger. Don was already angry enough for both of them. 'You're going to have to trust me,' he said.

Before Don could start again, Temple said, 'All right, everyone . . . as hard as it is right now, just calm down and let's consider this for a moment. O'Brien . . . if you think you can do it, if you really think you can do it . . . then I say — go do it. But if there's any doubt that you might endanger Mrs. Bishop, leave it. It's just not worth it. We'll do whatever Quillan says to get her back safely, and worry about the consequences afterwards.'

'That's fair enough,' said Bud. He looked at O'Brien, one eyebrow raised expectantly.

O'Brien sucked down a breath. *Do whatever Quillan says and get her back safely, and worry about the consequences afterwards.* It was sound advice, and by far the safer option. But it was also the option Quillan would expect them to take, and sometimes you had to take an entirely different course if you wanted to keep the other feller off-balance.

'I can do it,' he said softly.

★   ★   ★

Once full dark had cloaked the plains he'd headed for Sunrise, deliberately taking a roundabout route so that he could enter town from the north. He left his horse in the public corral, then headed for the alleyway beside the Sunflower Hotel via a series of scrappy back lots, there to keep watch on the saloon.

Now the lady pianist and the bartenders clattered out onto the boardwalk and with a few perfunctory goodnights, went their separate ways. Behind them, someone began to extinguish the first of the candle wheel chandeliers.

Belly tight, O'Brien broke cover and crossed Main, carefully checking the street to left and right as he went, but not seeing anything or anyone.

He came up on the porch just as Quillan's bouncer was about to hook the batwings back so that he could close the main door. He was a big, ugly man with the sweat-run face of a boxer who'd never quite dodged all the punches. He looked over the top of the batwings and, not recognizing O'Brien in the dim light, said, 'We're closed.'

'Not to me,' said O'Brien.

'Oh? An' who're you?'

'O'Brien,' he replied.

The bouncer stared at him for a moment more, then turned his head so that he could call over one big, slab-muscled shoulder.

'It's O'Brien,' he said.

From his table at the back of the saloon, Quillan looked up from a game of solitaire and called, 'Let him in.'

The bouncer stood aside and O'Brien pushed into the large room. A second bouncer was standing at the near end of the plank-and-barrel counter, finishing off what was left of that day's free lunch counter. He looked at O'Brien over the greasy pig's foot he was gnawing. His shotgun lay on the bar beside him. Newton was lounging down at the other end of the bar, smoking a black-paper cigarette and nursing his last drink of the night.

O'Brien stepped past the bouncer at the door, stopped when the man put a hand like a ham on his shoulder and tore his Colt from its holster. He shoved the gun into his waistband and then checked O'Brien for other weapons, quickly taking his jack-knife as well. Then he looked over at Quillan and said, 'Clean.'

'Alone, Freddie?' called Quillan.

The bouncer, Freddie, went out onto the porch and looked up and down the street for a long time. O'Brien held his breath. At last he stamped back into the saloon and said, 'Yup.' He let the breath go.

Quillan grinned. 'Well,' he called to O'Brien, 'ye certainly took your time gettin' here, mack. I thought you'd have come long before this.'

'I figured you'd prefer to discuss things in private,' O'Brien replied. He crossed the room toward the baize-topped table.

'That's very considerate of ye,' Quillan said easily, tossing his cards aside. 'But there's not really anything to discuss, is there?'

O'Brien shrugged. 'Bishop's willing to do business with you, if it means he gets his son's wife back. But he wants certain . . . guarantees . . . first.'

'Does he, indeed?'

'He'll be off the lease by dawn tomorrow,' said O'Brien. 'That's what you want, right?'

'It is.'

'And then you'll return the woman, unharmed.'

'That's the way it works.'

'Well, Bud wants that to be an end to it. All right? No more trouble. You leave him and his people alone, he'll leave you alone.'

'There's no profit in making any more trouble for him,' said Quillan. 'So tell him I'm happy to oblige. But don't include yerself in that, O'Brien. When this is all . . . concluded . . . we've got business, ye an' me.'

O'Brien nodded. 'That's about what I figured.'

'Is that it?' asked Quillan.

'No,' said O'Brien. 'I want to see the woman before I leave.'

'She's here, don't you doubt it.'

'I want to make sure she hasn't come to any harm.'

'She hasn't.'

'And I'm supposed to take your word for that?'

Quillan got that dangerous look again. 'Careful, mack. That's the second time you've called me a liar.'

'Well, that's too bad. Because my orders were to come here, get some guarantees and make sure Mrs. Bishop hasn't been harmed. If you can't show her to me and prove that, the deal's off. Bishop'll fight you all the way.'

Quillan said easily, 'Fight me, then.'

O'Brien shrugged, turned and started

back across the room. He got about halfway before Quillan called, 'Mack.'

He stopped, turned, saw that Quillan had stood up and come around the table. All at once the Irishman's right-side Cavalry Colt was in his hand and O'Brien's belly muscles clenched.

'You do know, a'course,' said Quillan, 'that you're in no position to make any demands a-tall?'

Forcing himself to stay calm, O'Brien raised his hands. 'That's what I plan to go back and tell Bishop.'

'No,' said Quillan. 'No. We'll have no more fightin', if we can help it. You'll see the lovely Kathryn, and you'll see that none of us have touched a hair on her sweet head. That's what you'll go back and tell Bishop.'

Coming slowly toward him, he used the barrel of the gun to indicate the staircase. 'Up you go,' he said. 'An' don't be gettin' any ideas, now.'

O'Brien turned and headed for the staircase, his spine itching. Newton took a drink and followed his progress through dark, edgy eyes. The bouncer at the near end of the bar continued to chew noisily on his pig's foot, his free hand never far from the shotgun on the counter.

O'Brien climbed the stairs, Quillan now right behind him. When they reached the gallery, O'Brien stopped. Quillan dug the long barrel of the Cavalry Colt hard against his spine and said, 'Keep moving. Third door along.'

O'Brien went along the gallery until he came to the door Quillan had indicated. Below, Newton and the two bouncers watched his every move, the half-dark saloon around them deadly quiet now. Then Quillan called, 'A visitor for ye, sweet Miss Kathryn. Someone who wants to make sure we haven't harmed ye.'

There was a key in the lock. Quillan told O'Brien to use it. He unlocked the door and it swung open with a soft, laddery creak.

The small room behind it was a typical crib — a bed and not much else.

A lantern, turned low on a cheap cabinet, showed him Kathryn sitting on the edge of the bed, her shadow thrown large up across the drawn drapes behind her. Her expression was flat and unreadable.

He looked at her and said, 'Are you all right?'

She nodded hesitantly.

'Have they hurt you?'

'No.'

'Satisfied?' asked Quillan.

Ignoring him, still focusing on Kathryn, O'Brien said, 'I'll tell Don you're all right. Then we'll get you out of here.'

Kathryn opened her mouth to say more, but never got the chance to reply.

'All right,' Quillan said briskly. 'Ye've seen her, seen she's all right. Now go back and tell Bishop he should be off that lease by first — '

Moving fast, O'Brien twisted and elbowed Quillan's gun-arm aside. Taken by surprise, Quillan's finger tightened on the trigger, the gun blasted and a bullet slammed up into the rafters.

By then O'Brien had dodged behind him, circled his left arm around Quillan's throat and was drawing his head back in a vicious chokehold, and as Quillan gasped and struggled, O'Brien used his free hand to tear the Colt from the Irishman's hand.

He rammed the barrel against the skin behind Quillan's right ear and barked, 'Not a move, any of you! Tell 'em, Quillan!'

Down below, Newton and the two bouncers had frozen in the act of reaching for their weapons. They stared up at the gallery, eyes spiking hate for O'Brien but aside from that, not knowing what to do for the best.

'Tell 'em!' hissed O'Brien.

He cocked the Colt's hammer for effect, and the *sni-sni-snick* it made was loud and scary.

'Stay where you are,' Quillan managed in a rasp.

'Get your hands up and move into the center of the room,' O'Brien added.

'You — Newton! You take your gun out real careful, fingertips only! That's the way . . . now put it on the bar. Steady, now . . . '

Newton did as he was told, then moved slowly to join the bouncers in the middle of the room, hands raised shoulder-high.

O'Brien took the gun away from Quillan's ear and stuck it in the small of his back. 'All right, Kathryn,' he called over his shoulder. 'We're getting out of here. You, down there! If anyone tries to stop us, I'll blow your boss's spine out through his belly, got it?'

Quillan struggled in his grasp, made an attempt to kick O'Brien in the shins. O'Brien tightened his chokehold until Quillan saw little flashes of light before his eyes and stopped.

'Kathryn,' he called again.

She came out through the doorway, looking scared. She looked down at Newton and the bouncers below, then at Quillan. Her mouth firmed up then, and with new resolve she pulled

Quillan's jacket aside and reached for his left-side Colt.

'Easy, girl,' said O'Brien.

'I'm all right,' she assured him.

She drew the gun. It looked more like a carbine in her small fists. Keeping her eyes on the three men below, she struggled to draw back the hammer.

'All right,' said O'Brien. 'Let's go.'

She looked at him then, and slowly brought the gun around so that it was pointed right at his face, and she said, very definitely: 'No.'

* * *

O'Brien looked past the gun, into her eyes, and knew then that he'd been had.

He thought, *Damn* . . . or words to that effect.

'Take that gun away from his back and let him go,' Kathryn said nervously.

For a long moment he didn't move.

She said, 'I mean it . . . '

He saw her finger whiten as she took

up first pressure on the trigger and grudgingly held up the gun, letting it dangle from his trigger finger. Quillan pushed away from him, turned, snatched the Colt and hit him alongside the head with the barrel. O'Brien went down to one knee, seeing stars, and heard the Irishman chuckle above him.

'Get up, mack,' he said, voice raspy and sore-sounding. 'I've got a feelin' you're wearin' an expression I'd like to see right now.'

Slowly, pretending that the blow had hurt him more than it actually had — though it had hurt plenty bad as it was — O'Brien straightened back up. When he looked at Kathryn she looked away from him.

'It's not what you think,' she said. 'I came here to — '

'Save it for Don,' he muttered.

'I — '

'We thought you'd been kidnapped,' he said tiredly. 'But that's what we were meant to think, wasn't it?'

'Well, let's have no doubts about it,'

said Quillan, chuckling some more. 'The lady came to me of her own free will. It appears she was somewhat ... aggrieved ... at how she'd been treated by the Bishops. Said as how she felt like she was invisible to 'em, like she just didn't count ... and how a man like meself might be more to her taste.'

O'Brien only looked at her, and under his scrutiny her expression hardened. 'Could you blame me?' she demanded, and the hatred in her made her look ugly. 'You saw how it was! I didn't even exist to Don! All he ever thought about was that damn lease — '

'The one he named after you, you mean?' O'Brien reminded her.

She waved that aside with the gun she still held. 'He didn't want a wife!' she spat. 'All he wanted was someone to cook his meals and warm his bed!'

'So you decided to switch sides and give Quillan his chance to take the lease, right?'

'I wised up,' she spat. 'And instead of judging me, you should thank me! I've actually done Don and Bud a favor. This way there'll be no more shooting. No one gets hurt.'

O'Brien looked at Quillan. 'So where does that leave us, Irish?' he asked.

Quillan grinned that insolent grin of his. 'I'll tell you where it leaves me,' he replied. 'With the chance I've been waiting for, to take over what promises to be the biggest oilfield for a thousand miles around, and live out the rest of me days like a king.'

'And Kathryn?'

'She'll be me queen, o' course,' he replied.

But the look in his green eyes added, *Until I get tired of her.*

His face changed then: the easy smile suddenly died, the lips clamped tight and he hooked his free fist into O'Brien's stomach. O'Brien bent at the waist, losing air and trying to drag it back into his lungs, and while he was doing that Quillan struck him a hard, downward blow.

O'Brien fell to his knees again,

knowing he was finished for sure now, because there was no way Quillan could let him go back to the lease and tell what he now knew to be the truth of the 'kidnap'.

Then, downstairs —

— a windowpane shattered.

Coming in to kick him, Quillan was momentarily distracted by the sound. It gave O'Brien just the chance he needed. He caught the Irishman's boot and pulled hard. Yanked off balance, Quillan grabbed for the banister rail, missed and slammed hard onto his back. O'Brien leapt on him, hit him a knockout blow in the face and ripped the Colt from his hand.

Down below, the bouncer who'd been eating the pig's foot grabbed his shotgun off the bar. At the shattered window, flame burst from the rifle barrel that had just broken the glass and the crash of a shot filled the room. The bouncer flew backward, discharging his shotgun into the ceiling as a well-placed .44/.40 punched him from this life into the next. He hit a table and fell, and his impetus shoved the table onto its side.

Upstairs, Kathryn screamed and threw herself at O'Brien from behind. He stood up with her clinging to his back and trying to club him with the Colt she still held. He did the only thing he could — he slammed back against the wall and the breath went out of her in a rush.

As she fell off him, he ran for the stairs.

The other bouncer, the one Quillan had called Freddie, had discharged one barrel of his Purdey side-by-side at the rifleman at the window. Now, turning to O'Brien, he stabbed the shotgun up ahead of him and pulled the double trigger again.

The left-hand barrel discharged with a roar like a burning devil, and O'Brien threw himself backwards even as the banister rail disintegrated.

At the same moment a gun blasted behind him. Flinching, he twisted at the waist, saw Kathryn trying to cock Quillan's second Colt for another shot at him.

To avoid that, he ran for the stairs again, made a reckless descent with the Cavalry Colt blasting the way ahead even as, below, Freddie finished reloading his weapon. Two bullets took Freddie in the chest, folded him like laundry and deposited him on the sawdust-covered duckboards, where he kicked a little, then lay still.

Reaching the foot of the stairs, O'Brien pulled up short and threw himself down behind the corpse even as Newton threw a shot at him from the far end of the bar. It punched into the bouncer, who only rocked unfeelingly with the impact.

O'Brien's return shot tore a long splinter out of the plank bar. Newton dropped out of sight.

The Cavalry Colt was empty. O'Brien tossed it aside and snatched his own Lightning from Freddie's waistband. From the corner of his eye he saw movement up on the gallery and quickly fired a shot up into the ceiling above Kathryn's position, to make her think twice about shooting at him again.

At the same moment Newton came up from behind the bar and fired another shot. O'Brien rolled, came up behind the overturned table, and heard the boom of the rifle firing in through the window again. He got his legs under him and started to shove the table forward, so that it shuddered and scratched its way toward Newton's position, gathering sawdust ahead of it.

Newton fired again: the bullet punched into but not through the thick wood. He fired twice more, then decided to cut his losses.

He leapt up and ran for the back door. Hearing the drum of his feet against the duckboards, O'Brien came up, snap-aimed, fired, missed.

Newton vanished out into the night, the back door slamming shut behind him.

All at once O'Brien grew aware of his own loud breathing and the fierce push of blood in his ears. He looked up at the gallery, where Kathryn was shaking Quillan, trying to bring him around with cries of, 'Hugh! Hugh!' Disgusted, he kept a careful eye on her as he walked back across the saloon and retrieved his jack-knife from Freddie.

'Hugh!' she yelled tearfully. 'Wake up!'

Deciding it would be more trouble than it was worth to drag her back to the lease, he peered over the batwings out into the street. The gunfire had attracted a scattering of late birds, but there was no sign of Newton.

He stepped out into the street, gun still in hand.

Vanishing into the alley beside the hotel, he cautiously worked his way down to the public corral. Harry Chamberlain was waiting for him when he got there, just as they had previously arranged. He still carried the rifle with which he had broken the saloon window and shot the hungry bouncer.

'Didn't go quite the way you

planned, did it?' he noted mildly.

'Nope.'

'So you got no more need for this here spare horse?' he said, nodding to the nervous saddle mount tethered to the top corral post.

'Nope.'

'Want me to go back an' arrest Quillan?' he asked. 'Charge of abduction? It'd keep him off your back.'

O'Brien shook his head. 'You couldn't make it stick. He'd deny it, and so would she. Hell, they'd end up swearing out a warrant for *my* arrest.'

'What a bitch,' said the lawman, thinking about Kathryn. 'As for Newton . . . I *knew* he'd hightail it! I still owe him for what he tried to do to Eddie.'

'You'll get another chance before this is over,' O'Brien assured him. Still keeping a wary eye on their surroundings, he toed in and swung across leather, then leaned over and offered his right hand. 'Thanks, Harry,' he said quietly.

'You asked me to back you,' Chamberlain said, shaking with him. 'That meant a lot to me — you showin' trust like you did.'

'Well, you backed me, all right. All the way.'

Chamberlain said nothing to acknowledge that, but was clearly pleased with the praise. 'Get on back to that lease,' he said roughly.

'I will. And you get on back to your office. The less Quillan knows about what you did here tonight, the better.'

Chamberlain raised a hand in farewell. 'I hear anythin', I'll be out to report it.'

O'Brien turned his horse toward the shadowy back lots. 'Obliged,' he said.

And meant it.

10

When Don spotted O'Brien approaching the lease without Kathryn in tow, he feared the worst. But in a way, the worst was still to come.

Hollow-eyed, Don, Bud, Temple and the wildcatters gathered on the edge of the moon-washed lease to watch his arrival. The tension in them was clear to see.

'What happened?' Bud asked when O'Brien finally drew rein and swung down. 'If you — '

O'Brien made no immediate reply. As Johnny Organ took the horse from him, he just put an arm around Don's shoulders and started leading him toward the dugout.

'What happened?' asked Don, his voice high, edgy. 'Where's Kathryn?'

When they were alone in the dugout, O'Brien told him.

Don's expression slackened, he swayed

a fraction, and his lips parted. 'No,' he said, his voice a harsh croak.

'I wish I could tell it differently, Don. But that's the way it was. The way it is.'

'I don't believe it!' Don snarled. 'You're lying!'

But the defeated slump of his shoulders, the chin-on-chest angle of his head, told a different story. Not only did he believe it: just like O'Brien, a part of him had half-expected it.

O'Brien started toward the door. 'I'll leave you alone for a while.'

'No,' Don replied sharply. 'No . . . you grab yourself some coffee. You've been beaten up and shot at and you look like hell.'

Without waiting to debate it, he opened the dugout door and went outside again. He stalked off into the darkness, looking neither left nor right.

O'Brien picked up the coffeepot and poured himself a cup. Behind him, Bud quietly filled the doorway.

'She ran out on him, didn't she?' he said softly.

'Uh-huh.'

'For Quillan?'

'For everything Quillan could give her,' O'Brien confirmed.

Bud punched the doorframe. 'I *knew* it! Deep down, I *knew* it!'

'You and Bud played your part in it too,' O'Brien reminded him.

Bud stiffened and started to deny it, then allowed his shoulders to drop. 'Maybe we did, at that. But still . . . '

O'Brien didn't want to discuss it anymore. 'Still think you can bring this well in before time runs out?' he asked to change the subject.

'If we can make up for the time we've already lost, yeah . . . we can. I'm sure of it. We *got* to be close to that oil now.'

'Then keep at it,' said O'Brien. 'And post two guards — Temple and any other man you think you can spare. Have them keep watch while the rest of us grab some sleep. And do me a favor, will you? Keep an eye on Don. Make sure he doesn't do anything stupid.'

'Too late for that,' Bud replied. 'The

stupidest thing he ever did was marry that bitch in the first place.'

He left, closed the door behind him. A few minutes later O'Brien went out to the trough and washed. Feeling fresher, though still sore from his beating, he went over to the tarpaulin-tent, flopped down on his bunk, tucked his Colt under the pillow and yet again found himself wondering what in hell was going to happen next, and what he was going to do about it. He closed his eyes and thought of Don, out there in the darkness, thinking about his woman and what she'd done to betray him.

Somewhere along the line he drifted into a shallow sleep.

He came awake with a start, not knowing why until he saw Temple standing frozen in mid-step in the tent entrance. The attorney looked startled — and when O'Brien saw that he had his Colt in hand and pointed Temple's way, he understood why.

'You're not an easy man to creep up on,' said Temple.

'What's wrong?' asked O'Brien, sitting up and sliding the Colt back into leather.

'Chamberlain's coming.'

'Alone?'

'Aside from that dog of his, yes.'

O'Brien got up. The sleep had refreshed him. Grabbing his hat, he followed Temple across the lease. The donkey engine was chugging steadily, the walking beam remorselessly clanking up and down, up and down, and Bud and Don were concentrating all their attention on the operation of the temper screw and augur stems.

Chamberlain drew rein at the edge of the lease. 'Trouble's comin',' he said without preamble.

'What does that mean?' asked Temple, uneasily.

'Quillan's buildin' an army. He's had men out since sun-up, offerin' gun wages to anyone who'll take 'em.'

'Has he had any luck?' asked O'Brien.

'Some. Lucky for you, most of those fellers are wildcatters. They won't fight against him, but they sure won't fight with him, neither. Not that it really matters.'

'Why not?'

'Because he's already got an army — he just wants a bigger one, is all.'

'I know he came in with a rough-looking crew,' said Temple.

'Well, he's also got a second bunch, just as rough, out on the plains, rustlin' cattle for him as a sideline — though I've never yet had a chance to prove it. The word I get right now is that he's pullin' 'em back into Sunrise, an' there can only one reason for that. He's gonna hit you hard, O'Brien — and for keeps.'

O'Brien exhaled. 'How sure are you about what he's planning to do?'

'About as sure as birth an' death.'

'All right. Thanks, Harry.'

The lawman's eyebrows rose. 'That's it? *Thanks?*'

'Well, what more do you want?'

'An invitation to stay on an' join the party might be nice.'

O'Brien shook his head. 'Your place is in town.'

'Hell with that,' said the lawman, urging his spaniel to leap down off his lap. 'You need all the guns you can get — an' mine's as good as anyone's.'

O'Brien smiled at him. 'It's better than most,' he said.

''Sides,' Chamberlain continued as he dismounted, 'we had an agreement, case you've forgotten. I'm gonna be in at the finish.'

O'Brien looked off across the meadow. 'He'll bide his time,' he muttered, trying to put himself in Quillan's boots. 'He'll make us wait, wear us down, then hit us tonight or first light tomorrow. It has to be after dark, else we'll see 'em long before they get here.'

An idea forming in his mind, he took out his old Hunter and checked the time. It was a little after ten o'clock.

'Might be possible,' he said softly.

'What are you talking about?' asked Temple.

'Tell the men what's happened and

what to prepare for,' he replied. 'Do what you can to build up some fortifications. I'll be back soon as I can.'

Temple froze. 'You're leaving us? *Now?*'

'I'll be back,' O'Brien replied. 'Marshal, you've got more experience with this kind of thing than anyone else here. You're in charge till I get back.'

After that there was no more time for talk. He hurried to the corral, caught up and saddled the blood-bay. Five minutes later he was heeling the horse north at a hard run.

⋆　⋆　⋆

He skirted Sunrise and kept trending north. He was taking a long chance and he knew it. But aside from going directly to The Christmas Tree and trying to settle this business man-to-man with Quillan, just the two of them, he was fresh out of ideas.

The morning wore on, gray and cheerless. He pushed the blood bay hard and hated doing it, but time was the thing now, and he only knew that he didn't have anywhere as much as he could use.

Then he began to spot cattle crazing on the poor, sickly-looking grass, and felt a stab of relief when he spotted the brand. A few miles on he came across two cowboys fixing a broken fence and angled toward them to get directions to the ranch itself. They eyed him with suspicion, but after a moment one of them made a terse gesture toward the east.

O'Brien nodded thanks and pushed on.

Twenty minutes later he reached his destination. The ranch was a long, single-story bunkhouse and cook-shack, a barn, stable and blacksmith's shop with two corrals, all set around what cowboys called the Big House — the place where the boss lived. As he rode into the yard and on toward the house — a modest clapboard-and-shake affair surrounded by a covered porch — the red glow of the forge inside the shop showed him the blacksmith, hammering a white-hot shoe into shape.

He was about twenty feet from the porch when the front door opened and a small, stocky man stepped outside with a slim, slightly shorter woman at his side. They watched him come, and when he was close enough Lon McPhail snapped his fingers and said, 'O'Brien, right? Judas Priest, man, I never expected to see *you* again!'

★ ★ ★

When O'Brien had been invited down and McPhail had ordered a young boy — his son, judging by the likeness between them — to take care of their visitor's horse, the rancher and the woman led him into the parlor. Here, McPhail said, 'This is that feller I was tellin' you about, Grace — the one who give me those swollen knuckles — which same I asked for — and damn near set fire to the whole territory.'

He laughed as he shook O'Brien's

hand. 'Never figured I'd ever punch a coffeepot!' Then he indicated the woman. She was small of frame, brunette, with a pleasant smile and good skin. 'This here's my wife, Grace,' he said.

Hat in hand, O'Brien nodded a greeting and said as how he was pleased to meet her.

'Coffee, Mr. O'Brien?' she asked.

'Thank you, ma'am.'

After she had left the room, McPhail's smile faded a little and he said, 'Come to take me up on my offer of work, have you? Well, that's — '

'Not quite,' O'Brien replied.

McPhail scowled. 'Then . . . ?'

In a few brief sentences he outlined the events of the past few days.

McPhail listened without interruption, then said, 'So what is it brings you here?'

'Quillan's planning to attack the Bishop well and take it by force,' he replied. 'He'll come tonight or first thing tomorrow. He wants that well, but more than that, he wants to make an example out of me and all the other folks out there.'

'And you want my help?'

Hating to have to ask, O'Brien said, 'Yes.'

'Hell, man, you've got some nerve!'

'What I've got,' said O'Brien, 'is an army coming to wipe out the people I signed on to protect.'

'That's *your* problem,' said McPhail. Then, moderating his tone a little, he added, 'Look, I'm sorry, but . . . I'd help if I could, but it's not my fight!'

'That's where you're wrong, Lon. Quillan doesn't just run Sunrise, he's also behind your rustling problem.'

McPhail's eyes narrowed. 'You got any proof of that?'

'The marshal's picked up enough hearsay to convince him.'

'Hearsay's not evidence.'

'I guess not. But when did your rustling start?'

McPhail hesitated a little before saying, 'Just after Quillan came in.'

'Coincidence, you think?'

'Likely not,' McPhail replied. 'But . . . I'm not a fighter, O'Brien. Hell, that's why I tried to hire you! I'm a rancher, and these men I employ, they're cowhands. Happen we came to help you, I'd likely lose some of 'em, maybe even get shot or killed myself . . . an' I don't aim to turn my wife into a widow just yet.'

O'Brien nodded. 'That's about what I figured,' he said, trying to mask his disappointment. 'But I had to ask. We're not going quietly. We can't. If Quillan wants that lease so bad, he's going to have to shed blood for every inch he takes.'

McPhail's wife came back into the room, carrying a tray. If she sensed any tension between the two men, she gave no sign. O'Brien stayed just long enough for coffee, then climbed back to his feet. 'I got to be moving on,' he said. 'Thanks for the hospitality, Mrs. McPhail.'

McPhail also rose and saw him out onto the porch, where he whistled and told the boy to fetch O'Brien's horse. 'I'm sorry,' he said again. 'I wish I could help, but out here I guess we mind our own business, an' only get involved when we have to.'

'That's what allows men like Quillan to move in and take over,' O'Brien pointed out. 'But don't worry, I get it.'

'So what will you do now?'

'The only other thing I can do. Go back to The Christmas Tree and brace Quillan man to man, just me and him. Maybe I can finish it that way.'

McPhail blanched. 'Are you crazy? That sonofabitch is like a blue streak with those guns of his! You honestly think you can take him?'

'I can't see any other way to avoid what'll happen if I don't.'

McPhail swallowed hard and put out his hand. O'Brien took it and they shook. The boy fetched O'Brien's horse and he took the reins and stepped up to leather. Gently, he touched his fingers to the brim of his hat and said, 'Be seeing you.'

'I hope so,' McPhail said softly.

O'Brien turned the blood-bay and rode

out, headed for Sunrise . . . and whatever awaited him there.

★   ★   ★

He'd played a long chance and it hadn't come off. All right. There was no sense crying over it. It was what it was . . . and it made his next course of action inevitable.

But did he have the speed to beat Quillan to the draw? He really didn't know. And even if he did, was there any guarantee that he would live long enough to celebrate his victory? Wherever he found Quillan, Newton wouldn't be far behind. And Newton wouldn't hesitate to shoot him from hiding.

If he could nail Quillan . . . if he could nail Newton . . . then maybe he had a chance. If not, it was over — for the Bishops, for Temple, for Congressman Norris . . . and for himself.

He'd been riding for the better part of an hour when he sensed that he was no longer alone in the scrubby border country. Slowing the horse, he twisted around and saw a group of riders on his back-trail, bunched-up about half a mile away and coming on fast.

He tensed, and the horse beneath him started to fidget nervously. Then the riders came closer, and he was finally able to identify their leader. Something inside him seemed to shift then, almost like a blossoming of hope.

A couple of minutes later McPhail raised his left hand to bring the three men behind him to a halt. O'Brien looked at them, saw that they were all armed, every man there — he recognized one of them as McPhail's blacksmith — wearing a set expression.

'Change your mind?' O'Brien asked, trying to keep the excitement out of his voice.

McPhail grinned, though the grin was a little sickly. 'After you left, I put it to the men,' he replied. 'An' these fellers here didn't figure it was right, lettin' you fight a battle that's as much ours as yours.'

'You know you'll be going up against forty men? Maybe more?'

McPhail swallowed again. 'We know,' he said.

The odds were still three or four to one against them. But they'd just gotten a little better than they'd been a few minutes earlier.

'All right,' said O'Brien, 'let's ride!'

11

It was late afternoon when O'Brien led his little army into the lease. With introductions made, McPhail and his men turned their horses into the corral and made themselves at home, while O'Brien made a quick tour of the lease with Chamberlain, Temple, Bud and Don. As ever, Chamberlain's dog padded along faithfully at the marshal's heels.

'We've set up tripwires across those gaps there, there and there,' said the marshal, pointing with a callused finger. 'They're tied off at one end right now, and each one's been buried, real shallow. When we know they're comin' we'll pull 'em tight an' secure 'em at the other end, and with any luck they'll trip any riders as they come in. Used the lumber to set up a couple of redoubts for us here and over yonder.

That'll catch any of the sons who make it past the tripwires in a crossfire. Also fortified that platform halfway up the derrick with some additional timber. Put a man or two up there an' it'll be like shootin' fish in a barrel.'

'You did good, Marshal.'

'Much as it pains me to say it,' said Bud, 'he did better than good.' He grinned at Chamberlain and said, 'Could be we *was* wrong about you . . . starpacker.'

For the first time, O'Brien felt they might just have a chance. With the defenses in place, all that remained was to wait for the Irishman and his men to show up. 'Still sure you can bring this well in on time?' he asked.

Bud hooked an elbow at Don, hoping to draw him out of the moody silence into which he had fallen, but Don took no notice. Bud said, 'We'll do it. We're well over four thousand feet now. If we was anyplace else, we'd have struck oil days ago. But it's there, I can feel it. Another yard, another foot — hell man, another inch — and we'll have it.'

'All right,' said O'Brien. 'Let's get everyone fed and in place. It's going to be a long night, but for now, we've done just about all we can.'

As Don walked away, O'Brien went after him. 'I know it's a hell of a question,' he said. 'But . . . are you okay?'

Don's expression was bleak. 'Oh, just dandy.'

There was no point in continuing the conversation, so O'Brien only clapped him on the arm and said, 'Well . . . check your weapons. We'll figure out where to position everyone after we've eaten.'

The meal was a rough-and-ready concoction of bacon fried in flour, and a stack of burnt soda biscuits. The only thing that could be said for it was that it was filling. Afterwards, O'Brien addressed his troops.

'Quillan'll come in quiet at first, just to check the lay of the land. Let 'em come. Keep quiet, keep still, let 'em think we're theirs for the taking. I'll signal you when they've pulled back again, and then you can pull the tripwires tight.'

Johnny Organ said, 'What's the signal?'

'Know what a mockingbird sounds like?'

'Uh-huh.'

'That'll be the signal.'

Next, he set about positioning his men where they would do the most good. He tried to post Chamberlain up in the crow's nest, where he figured the marshal would be out of the line of fire, but Chamberlain saw through that immediately. 'I'm too old for all that climbin',' he said. 'I'll stay down here with you.'

There was no time to argue about it. 'All right. Temple — you take the derrick.'

Not trusting himself to speak, Temple only nodded.

He placed his men in pairs behind the trough, behind the first redoubt, beneath the wagon and gave each group orders to take it in turns to sleep while one man kept watch. The odd man, the blacksmith, he placed in the engine house.

At last, Chamberlain shut the water spaniel inside the dugout and together he and O'Brien tried to make themselves comfortable behind the first redoubt. Each man checked his ammunition and the workings of his handgun and rifle largely by touch. Even through the gloom, however, O'Brien saw how the marshal's hands shook a little as he handled his gun.

'You going to be all right?' he asked quietly.

Chamberlain made a sound of impatience. 'I was all right last night, wasn't I?'

'*Are* you?' O'Brien persisted.

'Don't tell me you're still listenin' to all them stories about ol' Chamberlain? How he used to be one fine lawman till his nerve gave out on him? I'd'a thought better of you, O'Brien. Well, if it'll stop you frettin', ol' Chamberlain's nerve *didn't* give out on him. Never. Not a once.'

O'Brien paused. 'So what happened?'

Around them, the night darkened still further, and a cold breeze started pushing clouds across the moon. 'I got sick,' the marshal replied grudgingly. 'Noticed it in my breathin' at first — got winded easier'n I should've. Feet swelled up, hands too. Got so I could hardly grip a pistol. Then I started feelin' sick all the time, shaky like I was just now. Figured it was just old age creepin' up at first. Didn't really want to think anythin' else. Then I started passin' blood, an' I figured I better see a doctor.'

'What did he say?'

'That I had somethin' called diabetes. Ever heard of it?'

O'Brien ran the word through his mind, then shook his head.

'Well, I hope to God you never get it,' said Chamberlain, ''cause it's a bastard.'

'Couldn't the doctor help you at all?'

'Oh, he helped, after a fashion. Told me to throw in my badge and start watchin' what I et.'

'And did it work?'

'I'm better, sure. But it only took one person to see the way I used to shake sometimes for the word to get out that I'd lost my nerve. After that I was pretty much — '

He bit off suddenly, as the spaniel in the dugout started barking.

A moment later, O'Brien felt the ground under them begin to tremble.

'They're comin',' hissed Chamberlain.

O'Brien took up his Winchester.

The spaniel continued to bark for a further sixty seconds, then fell silent. O'Brien chanced a look above the barricade, saw no one, sensed nothing. Even the ground had stopped trembling.

'They've stopped,' said Chamberlain. 'Decided to come in on foot, jus' like you said.'

'Maybe.'

Five minutes passed, and still nothing happened. At length Chamberlain murmured, 'Pears that damn dog's as edgy as we are.'

O'Brien nodded. 'Get some rest, Harry.'

'Hell with that,' said Chamberlain. 'You get *your* head down. I'll handle things here — that's if you're happy to put your trust in such a feeble old man.'

'All right, all right.'

For Chamberlain's sake, he made a show of settling down, even though he knew sleep would be impossible. About ten minutes later he heard Chamberlain's slow, rhythmic breathing and opened his eyes again.

It was the marshal who'd dozed off.

The night passed slowly and the cold wind blew harder. Coyotes howled whenever the constant clouds thinned enough to let them see the moon. Two hours went by, at the end of which he once again sensed movement in the ground beneath them. Hardly daring to breath, knowing that everything hinged on the outcome of the fight ahead of them, he strained his eyes and ears, searching for some confirmation that Quillan's army was out there right now, and moving ever closer.

Stillness settled back over the plain.

Then, around three o'clock in the morning, the clouds finally cleared and the moon bathed the lease in cold white light.

And that was when O'Brien saw him.

He was a blocky man in a buttoned jacket, carrying a Winchester across his chest. He lingered on the southern edge of the lease, inspecting the place as close as he could in the poor light.

O'Brien reached out and clamped a hand over Harry Chamberlain's mouth. The marshal came awake with a muffled grunt. He looked into O'Brien's face for a second, then nodded.

The Quillan man — and he could be no one else — continued to study the layout of the lease. O'Brien wondered if the rest of his men had been alert enough to spot him, and would stick to their orders to stay out of sight.

Time passed as slow as molasses as the man continued to fix the layout of the lease in his mind. At length, he turned and vanished back into the darkness.

O'Brien released his breath. Pitching the sound low, he imitated the mockingbird's insistent trill, then waited. One by one, the tripwires were carefully tugged free of their covering of dirt and tied off about two feet above the ground.

After that it was back to waiting.

But not for long.

Fifteen minutes passed. Then the ground started trembling again.

O'Brien and Chamberlain exchanged a glance. This time there was something different in the sound, something that built and kept building until —

Quillan's men hit them from three sides. They came out of the darkness at a hard run, yelling fit to bust and shooting at anything that made a target.

O'Brien and Chamberlain hugged the ground as lead flew in every direction. Bullets drilled through the tarpaulin-tent, perforated the wagon's canvas bonnet and started tearing both to shreds. The side of the wagon was quickly pocked with holes, the glass window in the engine house door shattered, and waterspouts leapt from the trough. Then the lead riders hit the tripwires, and what followed was chaos.

They went down in a pile on all three sides, men tipping from saddles, startled yells mixing with the screams of falling horses, and O'Brien, coming up from behind the timber, bawled, 'Hit 'em!'

Quillan's three groups were each about fifteen-strong. O'Brien snap-aimed and fired into the nearest tangle of men and mounts, and beside him Chamberlain followed suit.

For the first few seconds it wasn't so much a battle as a slaughter — *flame and thunder*, as Quillan called a fight in which no holds were barred — but that was how it had to be if they were to stand any chance at all against such long odds.

The scene was repeated right across the lease — the chaos caused by the tripwire stretched between the redoubt and the dugout was a replay of that between the wagon and the shredded tent, and again between the tent and the derrick. Bud and Don, Johnny Organ and a McPhail man named Steve Brennan, and Temple, in his roost high above, started pouring fire into the suddenly unhorsed men. Two spun and dropped in unison. Another was flung backwards off his horse, having been shot in the cheek.

But the element of surprise was already gone. Reacting fast, the men in the second wave were already leaping their horses over the ropes, leaving the dead and wounded where they lay, crisscrossing each other in the cleared area at the center of the lease as they shot back at the muzzle-flashes of O'Brien's men.

Beneath the wagon, Johnny Organ sighted his Henry repeater on a rider in a pony skin vest and shot him twice. The first .44/.40 bullet knocked him off his horse. The second missed, but there was no need for it — the dying man fell beneath the hooves of the horse directly behind him and was quickly stomped to death.

Another Quillan man extricated himself from the pile-up between the tent and the derrick. He leveled his Colt at the second redoubt, behind which Bud and Don were firing carbine and shotgun rounds into the enemy. He was just about to shoot when a bullet gouged dirt out of the ground barely a foot away. He looked around, then looked up, saw Temple shooting from the derrick platform and threw a shot up at him. Temple flinched back behind the cover of the plank barricade and the Quillan man ran for the cover of one of the legs of the derrick.

Alerted by the exchange, Don immediately saw what he was planning to do — to fire up at Temple from directly below his position, and quickly spun with the shotgun against his hip. The weapon boomed and the Quillan man was hurled backwards in a jumble of minced flesh.

Nate Newton, keeping to the edges of the lease while everyone else fought the battle for him, spotted O'Brien behind one of the makeshift redoubts and took aim with his Remington single-action Army .45. He was just about to squeeze the trigger when his attention was taken by the dog in the dugout. As he looked that way, he saw the dog alternately leaping up at the half-glass door and scratching furiously at the lower panel, as if trying to get out.

Contempt for the animal made Newton's whiskery mouth buckle, and he threw two shots into the doorway. The second shattered the glass, and he was rewarded by a frightened yelp from the dog.

At the second redoubt, meanwhile, Chamberlain saw what he'd done and muttered, 'Eddie.' Then, consumed by hatred, he stood up and fired his rifle. The shot missed its target, but came close enough to make Newton turn back toward the redoubt.

Growling Newton's name, Chamberlain broke cover and charged as best he could across the lease. O'Brien yelled for him to stay put, but the order was lost in the roar of battle.

Halfway across the lease, the marshal pulled up quick as a Quillan man galloped right across his path. He turned, took aim and shot the passing man in the spine. Then it was back to Newton.

Seeing the marshal coming at him, Newton looked to left and right for an escape route, decided he didn't have one and dropped into a gunfighter's crouch. He brought his Remington up, but by now Chamberlain was close enough to hurl his rifle at him. Newton flinched, and that bought Chamberlain enough time to hook his own big Remington from leather.

Even as Newton took aim again, the marshal fanned his gun, riddling Newton's upper chest with three .44s. With a scream, Newton went up on his boot-tips, his face contorted with agony. He seemed to hang there for a moment, until Chamberlain shot him one more time. Then twisted around and slapped the dirt.

Standing over the body, making sure Newton was deader than yesterday, the marshal muttered, 'Steal my dog, would you?'

Above the battle that raged around him, he heard Eddie barking and scratching frantically at the bullet-riddled door. He stumbled into the dugout, dropped down and started reloading with shaking fingers while Eddie, mercifully unharmed, licked at his face.

O'Brien was reloading too. But although they'd given a good account of themselves — better than he'd had any right to expect — the fight was starting to go badly. Even as another Quillan man pitched from his horse and O'Brien came back up firing, he saw Johnny Organ roll sideways beneath the wagon, his ebony face twisting as he clutched a bloody patch on his upper left arm.

Behind the trough, McPhail saw how things were going as well, and broke cover to send a withering fusillade into some milling Quillan men nearby. The puncher with him followed his example and added to the volley. Then, hit, McPhail dropped to one knee, even as the puncher next to him took a bullet in the throat.

Beside Johnny Organ, Steve Brennan had come out from beneath the wagon, intending to take the fight to the enemy. He was shot almost immediately, slammed up against the Conestoga's sideboards and slid down into a sitting position, eyes wide and unblinking.

Beside Don, Bud went a little crazy, firing and levering his carbine as fast as he could, pumping round after round into Quillan's gunnies. The din reached a crescendo as men screamed, horses whickered, the dog barked, and once again the ground trembled to the pounding of horse hooves.

All they could do was keep up a steady, relentless volley of fire. There could be no science to it, just cut them down and keep cutting them down any way possible, and it was a rotten but necessary business in which the only reward was survival.

And then, right out of nowhere . . .

Quillan.

Like Newton, the Irishman had held back as long as he could, letting everyone else do the fighting for him, and now that he sensed it was almost over, he came charging in astride a spirited hammerhead gray to rouse his troops for one final push.

'Get 'em!' he bawled, jabbing one of his Colts here, then there to punctuate his orders. 'You, Franklin! Use the dynamite I gave ye an' blow that feckin' engine house! Lacey — gather some men an' charge that damn timber! I want them all dead!'

O'Brien got Quillan in his sights and squeezed the trigger. The bullet missed and hit Quillan's saddle horn instead, shattering wood before ricocheting off the metal base beneath it. Startled, Quillan twitched, reined his horse around and returned fire.

By then O'Brien had turned his

attention to the man called Franklin, who had dismounted and was preparing to throw a sputtering stick of dynamite at the engine house. But the blacksmith, Allen Cobb, was already onto him. He fired a Winchester at the man, once, twice, thrice, four times: and the volley threw Franklin backwards, still clutching the dynamite. A second later he vanished in a fireball.

The detonation made the ground shake so hard that O'Brien almost lost his footing. He saw that the other man Quillan had singled out — Lacey — was turning his mount and yelling as he prepared to charge the redoubt with seven or eight men right behind him.

More movement, away to O'Brien's left — then Chamberlain was back beside him, having retrieved his rifle en route.

'This is it!' he yelled, and drew himself up to his full height, ready to take as many of the enemy with him as he could.

He planted himself solidly and shot

at Lacey, but missed because the ground was still heaving beneath him. He racked in another load, steeling himself against the wall of fire Lacey's men were setting up, and fired again. This time he hit Lacey in the knee, and the man's free hand flashed to the wound. As the rest of his men weaved around him, surging closer with every second, Chamberlain fired repeatedly into their ranks until his rifle clicked empty.

Still they came.

And still the ground heaved and roiled underfoot.

And then —

A roar just like a twenty-one gun salute split the pre-dawn apart and the ground gave one final, sickening lurch. O'Brien thought, *They're using more dynamite*.

But then another sound added to the ear-blasting din; a painful, grinding, *wrenching* sound, and the oncoming riders, sensing that something new and potentially disastrous had happened, drew rein, turned in their saddles, looked around.

O'Brien did likewise, just as the derrick shuddered visibly and the drill pipe at the center of that intricate web of beams and cables suddenly lifted up, as if propelled by some unstoppable force beneath it.

Unable to believe his eyes, Chamberlain muttered, 'Criminy.'

The drill pipe shot high into the sky like a ballistic rocket that hadn't been used since the Civil War. Cables snapped and flapped before falling back to earth. And behind the drill pipe there came a great, growling arc of dirt, limestone, rock . . .

. . . and oil.

A flash of insight then told O'Brien what must have happened; that Lacey's dynamite had finally shattered the last inch, half-inch, quarter inch of crust that lay between oil and Bishop's drill bit. Now, the force with which the oil was released was a sight to behold.

It soared high into the dawn-gray sky

and then, reaching its zenith, began to flood back down over the plain. The fight forgotten, the sight of the drill pipe tumbling back to earth a quarter-mile away captivated Quillan's men, who suddenly found themselves struggling to control their frightened mounts . . . and rethinking where this new turn of events left them.

Whatever they'd hoped to achieve here . . . it was over now — Bishop had brought the well in, the man they themselves had signed on with had failed in his objective, and not one of them cared to chance fighting on for a lost cause in such potentially hazardous conditions.

To the south, puddles began to fill, thick, black and glutinous. The roar of the downpour was close to deafening. Men and horses on that side of the lease were covered now in glossy black oil that stank worse than rotten eggs, and as if by mutual consent they decided to cut their losses, dig in their spurs and start back toward Sunrise.

It was a sentiment the rest of them shared.

Chamberlain raised his rifle to send a few shots after them, but O'Brien yelled, 'No!'

The marshal looked at him.

'One spark and the entire lease'll go up!'

Even as Chamberlain nodded his understanding, a new voice screamed:

'Help!'

Quillan's men were well and truly in retreat now. All that remained on the lease were the bodies of men and mounts and a scattering of riderless horses. Then Don looked up, realized that the sudden eruption of oil had bowled Temple over — that the attorney had fallen and was now hanging half-way out of the derrick platform and clinging to oil-soaked timbers for dear life.

Thrusting his shotgun at Bud, he hurried to the derrick and started scaling it as fast as he could. The sky was still brightening slowly with the coming dawn, but he knew instinctively where to put his hands and feet, which was just as well, given that the force of the released oil had weakened the structure and given it a drunken lean that was increasing by the second.

He was halfway to the platform when a shot rang out. Startled, Don lost his footing, found himself clinging to the timbers by his hands only. But he hadn't been the shooter's intended target.

O'Brien felt the bullet zip past his face, and turning at the waist, saw Quillan sitting his skittish gray horse in the shadows just beside Newton's corpse, a Winchester held to his shoulder. He brought his Colt up even as the Irishman prepared to take a second shot.

O'Brien, figuring that his own shot would be unlikely to ignite any oil on that side of the lease, got him dead in his sights and pulled the trigger.

The Colt's hammer clicked on an empty chamber.

Quillan, meanwhile, was taking up first pressure on his second shot when something black and lithe blurred out of the dugout and went for the gray's hooves — Eddie.

Taken by surprise, the horse started crow hopping, and Quillan almost lost his seat. As the dog continued to savage the gray's cannon and fetlock, O'Brien worked the ejector rod, plugged in reloads, snapped the loading gate shut and took aim again.

Swearing, Quillan flung the rifle at the barking spaniel, gathered his reins and twisted the horse away to the north at a gallop the wounded animal couldn't hope to sustain.

As Bud finally reached the crow's nest, slipped in oil, righted himself and hurriedly hauled Temple back to relative safety, O'Brien threw himself over the redoubt, caught up one of the raiders' horses, which had tried to bolt but ended up stumbling on its trailing reins. He hit the saddle, turned the horse and went after Quillan at a reckless run.

The derrick continued to slip ever closer to the horizontal, still gushing oil everywhere, but Bud continued helping Temple down to the ground foot by foot.

The new day was lightening at last, but too slowly to afford O'Brien anything more than a vague outline of the country ahead, and the rider who had somehow managed to push his injured horse to the far side of the meadow.

The horse would go no further, though. O'Brien saw Quillan giving it his spurs, but the stubborn animal only stood there, his injured leg held up to take some of the pressure off it.

Quillan leapt from the animal's back. He was in such a fury that O'Brien saw him actually punch the horse. Then he was racing for the slope and the cover of the black walnut that studded its crest.

O'Brien, mouth firming, shoved his Lightning tight into leather and went right after him.

He passed the gray and was halfway up the slope when he spotted a sputtering light against the dawn sky, shedding sparks in a wide, lazy arc as it sailed toward him. He recognized it at once — the lit fuse on a stick of dynamite — and immediately yanked his mount hard to the left to avoid it.

The stick ran out of fuse while it was still about twenty feet above him. When it blew it turned dawn into day and the shockwave threw O'Brien and the horse beneath him sideways by a good dozen feet.

The horse came down hard, with a shrill neigh, and rolled over. O'Brien had thrown himself from the saddle long before that, but still hit hard enough to bring the pain of his healing ribs screaming back to life.

The horse, shocked by the fall, clambered up, jogged a little sideways, until the reins caught around its forelegs. Then it lifted its head so they cleared the ground and trotted away.

'Come an' get it, ye sonofabitch!' yelled Quillan, hidden on the far side of the ridge.

He threw another stick of dynamite.

Though breathless from the fall, O'Brien

pushed himself up and sprinted for the ridge. The dynamite hit the ground about ten feet behind him, bounced . . . and blew.

The shockwave picked him up and smashed him down thirty feet further up the slope. He blacked out for a moment — at least he thought he did — and when he pushed back to his feet, he realized that his balance had been shot to hell.

A persistent, high-pitched whine in his ears also told him that he'd been rendered deaf.

Damn!

Around him the slope tipped and tilted and though he tried to stand he quickly fell back to his knees.

'Ye've damn near cost me everything,' Quillan yelled, unaware that O'Brien couldn't hear a word he said. 'But I'm not finished yet!'

O'Brien screwed his eyes tight shut, opened them again, and was relieved to see that the world didn't spin quite so much anymore.

On hands and knees, he clawed his way laboriously toward the summit, finally rolled into the cover of the black walnut. The ground in front of him suddenly lit up and stretched his shadow long ahead of him — it was the only way he knew that Quillan had hurled a third stick of dynamite that had landed behind and below him.

Drifting smoke gave the slope the smell and appearance of a battlefield.

Struggling with the disorientating effect of the temporary deafness, he forced himself to think. Quillan, a dynamite man from way back, would know better than to keep his blasting caps and dynamite together until he was ready to use them. That meant he'd have to take a cap, push it gently into the gelatinous dynamite and then attach a fuse before he could use it. On top of that, he'd then have to fray the end of the fuse with his thumbnail in order to make it easier to light when he put a match to it —

And all that would take time.

Another stick turned end over end through the sky, fuse sputtering and sparking. It hit the slope six or seven yards away. Nothing happened immediately. Then —

It blew with a mighty roar O'Brien never heard.

But this was his chance. Clawing his way up the trunk, trying to keep a rough timetable of Quillan's actions in his mind, he stumble-ran from tree to tree. About a hundred feet to his right, Quillan was hunkered in the cover of some buttonbush, trying to light another stick of dynamite from a match that refused to strike. He had no idea O'Brien was already moving into position to attack him from behind.

O'Brien drew in a breath and kept moving, down on hands and knees again, still weaving like a drunk and trying to keep quiet even though he had no idea just how much noise he was making.

At last the match struck, and Quillan held the flame to the frayed tip of his fuse and threw the stick of dynamite out of the trees and onto the slope below. Another blinding flash sent the shadows reaching and told O'Brien that it had detonated.

At last he made it to some scrub no more than a dozen feet from Quillan's position. Quillan peered through the buttonbush, down the slope, searching for O'Brien's body, or what was left of it. Not seeing it, he exposed himself a little more.

O'Brien tensed his legs, ready to spring up and make a run for him while he was distracted. But just as he was about to make his move, Quillan, realizing at last that O'Brien was no longer down below him, and was in all probability right up here in the trees with him, made a move of his own.

He turned and started north at a jog.

And that was when O'Brien hit him.

His balance still shot, all he could do was throw himself at Quillan so that they collided, and the Irishman staggered backwards.

O'Brien was on him at once. Again, there was no science to it, he just threw himself at the Irishman and hoped that his weight would knock the fight out of him.

Quillan gasped but wriggled like an eel beneath him, finally pushing O'Brien off and over. Then it was Quillan's turn — he landed heavily on O'Brien and immediately started throttling him.

Movements still clumsy, O'Brien latched onto Quillan's wrists and tried to break the other man's stranglehold. His face screwed up with effort and his teeth showed white against his copper skin, but Quillan wasn't about to give an inch. He sat up on O'Brien, fingers digging hard into his flesh, nails breaking skin, knees pinning O'Brien's biceps firmly to the ground.

In desperation, O'Brien brought both knees up, kicked him in the spine, and that gave him the chance to free himself and shove Quillan aside.

They both leapt to their feet — Quillan was faster — and then went at it again, toe-to-toe, hammering at each other, blocking when they could, soaking up the pain when they couldn't, and after a minute of that they were both sweating and gasping, almost clinging to each other just to stay upright.

Still they struggled fiercely, each man trying to throw the other to the ground to give him the advantage, but then the ground went out from under them and O'Brien realized dimly that they were rolling down the far slope.

The descent lasted hours and was probably only seconds, and without warning they suddenly came to a halt near the oily, rock-ringed waterhole O'Brien had noted on his first trip out to the well. Quillan brought his knee up into O'Brien's chest, and O'Brien, his ribs flaring with pain, fell backwards. Quillan, himself exhausted by their fight, stumbled backwards himself, until twenty feet separated them.

Quillan's face, sweat-run, smeared with blood, green eyes alight with the unholy pleasure he was taking from this contest between them, swept back the folds of his frock coat and went for his Colts.

Surprise froze his features when he realized they weren't in their holsters — that they must have slipped free during their headlong plunge down the slope.

Down on his hands and knees, O'Brien saw as much as if through a haze.

Ponderously he slid his Lightning from its holster. Quillan watched him with fury mounting inside him, knowing the distance between them was too great, that O'Brien would shoot long before he could cover even half the ground between them.

With an effort that brought more sweat to his face, O'Brien aimed the Colt unsteadily and pulled the trigger.

More by luck than design, the slug clipped Quillan's shoulder. The pain was searing, but the wound itself would never qualify as serious. It pushed the Irishman back another step, and he lost his footing, slipped into the waterhole behind him with a chill splash of sound. He almost lost his balance completely, recovered —

— and froze.

O'Brien was leaning over. The fight and the fall had cost him practically everything. Deaf and disoriented, his stomach churning, he knew he was going to puke at any moment and that nothing he could do would stop it —

He threw up.

Seeing him down like that made Quillan pause, ankle-deep in the water. A moment later, a grin that was more like a snarl split his face. 'Look at the sorry state of ye, man,' he said. 'Ah, O'Brien, I'm gonna enjoy this, I really am.'

He reached into his pockets, brought out his last stick of dynamite. O'Brien forced his head up, saw the Irishman quickly cap and fuse the explosive with the facility of long practice.

Except there were two Quillans now, one image overlapping the other.

The Irishman fumbled in his pocket for a match.

Struggling with all the strength that remained to him, O'Brien brought the Colt up again. The gun wavered all over the place and Quillan chuckled, because this man who had ruined everything for him was no longer a threat.

'See ye in hell, ye langer!' he yelled.

As he struck the match on his thumb, O'Brien pulled the trigger and flame shot from the Lightning's short barrel.

His bullet flew low, missed its target completely.

But it struck the rocks that fringed the waterhole, and as lead met rock and whined off into the new day, it caused a spark.

And one spark was all it took.

The gas in the pond ignited with a harsh *whoof* of sound, and the fireball that followed consumed Quillan in an instant. He might have screamed, but if he did, it was lost beneath the sudden, greedy crackle of flames that engulfed him.

An instant later, the dynamite he'd been holding went off, and that drowned out everything else. A black-bellied ball of orange flame roiled skyward, and beneath it the blast left an airless vacuum that effectively smothered the fire before it could spread.

Thrown backward by the blast, O'Brien lay still for a moment, catching his breath, then rolled over, pushed back to his hands and knees and looked at the water.

In the growing day, steam rose sluggishly from its rippling surface. And in the middle of the waterhole, something black and red that could no longer be recognizable as a human being, lay all that remained of Hugh Quillan.

12

He passed out for a while after that, and when he came to again, he was surprised to hear his own labored breathing above the sound of birdsong. He told himself he might just survive after all.

Feeling older than his years, he took one last look at the thing in the waterhole, then climbed slowly back up the slope and through the trees, where he quickly spotted Quillan's hammerhead gray grazing quietly beside the horse he had taken to pursue it. Whispering nonsense, he got close enough to the horse and then hauled himself up into the saddle and rode back to the well. The gray followed on at a slow, limping gait.

When he rode in, the well — he doubted it would ever be referred to as the *Kathryn* again — was still littered with Quillan men and dead horses. But clearing up would have to wait. As Harry Chamberlain helped him toward the dugout, and Eddie came out to greet him with wagging tail, he heard — actually heard — Bud yelling something about capping the well.

Of course, no one had escaped unscathed. Everyone had scratches and cuts and other assorted hurts. McPhail had been wounded, but not badly. Neither was Johnny Organ's injury likely to prove fatal, though it would certainly sting like a bitch until it healed. But they'd lost Steve Brennan and a second McPhail man whose name had been Claude Yarbrough, and O'Brien felt their loss keenly, because those men had elected to fight when they could as easily have turned their backs and gone on living.

Capping the well was a job in itself, and involved the careful drilling of what Bud called relief wells, to take some of the pressure off the main one. It took weeks before the flow of oil was finally staunched, and Don told him that they had probably lost two thousand barrels of oil in the interim.

During that time, of course, came the funerals of McPhail's men, who were buried within sight of the Jenner brothers in the Sunrise cemetery. A number of townsfolk turned out to pay their respects, as indeed did Elijah Graves himself. In the wake of Quillan's attack on the Bishops, the old rancher had felt it necessary to call a meeting with the town's more influential inhabitants. The *Sunrise Journal* carried his apology for Quillan's activities, and a promise to wildcatters, townsfolk and the surrounding ranchers that from now on, things would be much different in Sunrise. Just to prove it, he levied a tax on all the businesses in town, which would pay to hire some deputies for Harry Chamberlain.

Chamberlain was quick to ask O'Brien if he fancied sticking around for a while, until he could find more permanent deputies, but O'Brien declined. The old marshal wasn't surprised: he'd heard that O'Brien never stayed in any one place for long. With the Bishop well capped and now in full production, the two men shook hands, and then O'Brien gave the water spaniel one last scrub of the ears before mounting up and riding on.

He hadn't gone more than a hundred yards when he saw a somewhat toil-worn Kathryn Bishop clearing tables at the same eatery he and Bud Bishop had patronized the day of the dog fight. He drew rein and watched her for a moment, and was just about to move on when she sensed him there and looked up.

'What do you want?' she asked.

'Nothing.'

She tried to hide her disappointment. 'Don didn't send you, then?'

He raised an eyebrow. 'What would he send me out here for?'

She shrugged. 'I don't know. Maybe he figured he couldn't live without me.'

O'Brien couldn't help it: he laughed. 'It's more likely he figured he could never live *with* you.'

'He said he didn't want me back,' she confirmed. 'But I didn't believe him. He came to see me, gave me seventy dollars. All he had until they start turning that oil into cash, he said. Told me to get out of Sunrise and never let him see me again.'

'But you're still here.'

'And so are they,' she replied, and made a vague gesture with the wet cloth in her left hand. 'Look at them, O'Brien. Ragged men, just about as poor as Job's turkey. But each one carryin' a dream . . . a dream of strikin' it rich.'

'And when one of them does,' guessed O'Brien, 'you'll be there.'

'I'll be there,' she nodded. 'Only the next man won't be like Don, married to the oil business. The next one'll sell out to the highest bidder and then we'll go see the world together, and it'll be like Sunrise never existed.'

She eyed him more closely then. 'And you?' she asked. 'Where are you headed, now it's over?'

'Well, I gave it considerable thought,' he replied. ''Fact, I stayed up the whole of last night, just pondering it. And you know what I decided, Kathryn?'

'What?' she asked.

He leaned sideways out of the saddle and answered confidentially, 'Anywhere the air smells a little cleaner than it does around you will suit me just fine.'

Not waiting to see the expression on her face, he turned the blood bay north and rode out.

And behind him, the drills on the far side of town kept *thump . . . thump . . . thumping.*

We do hope that you have enjoyed reading this large print book.

Did you know that all of our titles are available for purchase?

We publish a wide range of high quality large print books including:
Romances, Mysteries, Classics
General Fiction
Non Fiction and Westerns

Special interest titles available in large print are:
The Little Oxford Dictionary
Music Book, Song Book
Hymn Book, Service Book

Also available from us courtesy of Oxford University Press:
Young Readers' Dictionary
(large print edition)
Young Readers' Thesaurus
(large print edition)

For further information or a free brochure, please contact us at:
Ulverscroft Large Print Books Ltd.,
The Green, Bradgate Road, Anstey,
Leicester, LE7 7FU, England.
Tel: (00 44) **0116 236 4325**
Fax: (00 44) **0116 234 0205**

NIGHT TRAIN TO LAREDO

Roy Patterson

Visiting Chandler Crossing to take part in its famed poker tournament, Ben Garner finds himself flush with success, and a huge wad of cash. Before he can celebrate, however, he is robbed on the way to his hotel. Desperate and confused, he is suddenly confronted by a mysterious and beautiful woman named Molly Walker. Her offer of a large fee to act has her guard and travel with her on the night train to Laredo seems too good an opportunity to pass up. But is this luck, or misfortune?